THE GIFT

Books by Kathryn Elizabeth Jones
A River of Stones
Parable Series

> Conquering Your Goliaths: A Parable of the Five Stones
>
> Conquering Your Goliaths: Guidebook
>
> The Feast: A Parable of the Ring
>
> The Gift: A Parable of the Key
>
> The Parables of Virginia Bean

Heaven 24/7

> Living in the Light

Marketing Your Book on a Budget
Susan Cramer Mysteries

> Scrambled
>
> Sunny Side-Up
>
> Hard Boiled
>
> Over Easy

Brianne James Mysteries

> Tie Died
>
> Buckled Inn

The Space Adventures of Aaden Prescott

> Light*Shade*
>
> Light*Descending* – Spring 2019
>
> Light*Source* – Fall 2020

Mooseberry Mooseberry Gooseberry Pie

THE GIFT

A Parable of the Key

Book III

KATHRYN ELIZABETH JONES

Idea Creations Press
www.ideacreationspress.com

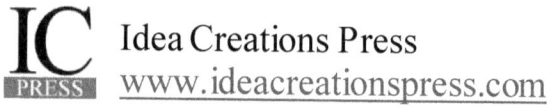

Idea Creations Press
www.ideacreationspress.com

This is a work of fiction. Any resemblance of characters to actual persons, living or dead, is purely coincidental.

Library of Congress Control Number: 2015948992

ISBN-13: 9780996665728

Printed in the U.S.A.

DEDICATION

A big thank you to my beta readers:

Joan Tolman

Tricia Leslie

Carolyn Tolman

Bethany Wursten

And, as always, to my husband and number one cheerleader, Doug

Preface

In The Feast: A Parable of the Ring, Virginia sought for what she wanted most, a child, and got her. She strengthened her marriage with Richard, and learned even more about Listening, Trust, Optimism, Tenacity and Constancy through the trials and joys of bringing a new life into the world. But life isn't always what you expect. And the stones, well-meaning as they are, can't begin to create the person you want to be (especially a person like Virginia is) if you no longer have the courage to really live their teachings.

Like now, for example.

Kathryn Elizabeth Jones

The Beginning

Beatrice was 9 months old when the key turned for Virginia. The summer leaves were just beginning to dry, preparing themselves for yet another fall and heavy winter in Idaho Falls, Idaho, and the little babe Virginia had finally managed to bring into this world had left it too soon.

No real cause. No real solution. But crib death was like that. "Don't turn her on her belly." "Don't put stuffed animals in her bed." "Don't smoke."

Well, she hadn't done any of those things and the baby girl that she'd waited for, for so long, was under the cold earth, never again to reach out her tiny little hands.

God was cruel.

No, that was the wrong thing to say.

God was...

She didn't know what God was. And she didn't know if she'd truly ever believe him again.

Richard was smart. He went to work. Struggled with the doughnuts and cupcakes that she still made for the tiny shop they'd finally managed to purchase away from the grocery store. He was smart because he kept himself busy, like a tall elf in Santa's shop, doing the busy stuff so the doughnuts could be delivered on time to the smiles of every heavy, needy customer.

All of her thoughts were negative now - the size of the customers, the way the air blew through the bottom of the front door in a sort of chilled whirr, the remembrance of icicles that would soon be dangling from the rooftop of their tiny home, like sharp knives penetrating her heart.

***

It would soon be Christmas.

And it wasn't fair. In spite of all she knew about God, all that he'd taught her, all that he'd shown her in the birth of their baby Beatrice, he had taken her daughter home. With so many children already, probably catering to his every need, he had taken her baby home. He had taken her home!

She sat, as she did most days since Beatrice's death two months ago. She hadn't put away any of the baby things, or taken down the crib. She couldn't touch the crib. She was lonely, sad and angry. She didn't know what to do with her pain, except cry.

Beatrice. What a beautiful little girl she'd been. She liked music, and when Richard danced with her, she'd smile, her first tooth protruding through her gums, like a tiny jack-o-lantern with a light inside.

It wasn't like Beatrice to cry. She was more likely to smile and giggle and drool.

She wore pink, of course. And Virginia had put her in fluffy dresses with pink bows and matching booties. She'd read her stories about princesses and queens and handsome strangers. Nights were filled with feedings and cuddling, and playing "This Little Piggy..." but that night...

Tears spilled down Virginia's cheeks. They'd replaced the couch that had sported the hole from the rock of trust. But now, even though their newfangled red couch was perfect in form and stability, she needed that hole; yes, somehow that hole would have soothed her soul.

She still had the stones; had kept the stones for these few years since she'd first walked with God. They were still with her, even now, as she sat on the couch and looked up at them on the mantel.

Listening...Trust...Optimism...Tenacity...Constancy... So close and yet so far away.

She couldn't even think, let alone stand to take the first one in her hands and listen to God. She wondered what he would say...

"I needed her..." "She's a sweet girl..." "You'll have another child..."

But she couldn't think about having another child, and she couldn't think about herself, and she couldn't think about Richard. Or God.

Richard...

***

"Virginia?"

Virginia was still sitting on the red couch when he approached. It was 7:30 p.m. and she still hadn't made lunch for herself or dinner for her husband.

11

"Yes?" She looked up at him and tried to smile.

He sat beside her. "How are you doing?" he asked, stroking her blonde hair though it was matted.

"Fair, I guess. You?"

"We had a big sale today. Sold almost all of the pink cupcakes." His arm reached around her back. "Would you like to go out to eat tonight?" he asked. "There's a great restaurant that's just opened up."

"Where?"

"Practically up the street." He forced a smile. "Italian."

She forced her own smile. "I guess it wouldn't hurt," she said.

"Tell you what. You get ready and I'll clean up a bit of the dishes..."

"Thanks." She stood and retreated to the bedroom, trying not to look at her daughter's old room across the hall. But she felt it nonetheless, would always feel her daughter within the room across from her own as if her she was still with them.

Changing from her pajamas, she slipped into a pair of jeans and a gray t-shirt, reached for a sweater, some socks, and finally a pair of tennis shoes, hoping but not really caring, that the place was casual.

Richard smiled over at her when he saw her. He'd almost finished loading the dishes in the dishwasher - only a pan remained. "What about your hair?" he asked, turning back to the sink.

She ran her fingers through the tangled strands. "I'll be back in a minute." She turned down the hall to the bathroom. Per his request, she brushed through her hair, and pulled the long strands into a ponytail, trying to avoid her reflection. But it was no use. Her eyes looked like giant red balls, puffy and swollen like the back end of a baboon. She looked sickly, and it pained her to see what she'd become.

Was it ever going to be different? Would she ever feel happy again? Or would this sadness drag on, hanging onto her every limb as she went about her day?

"Ready?" Richard had been standing at the bathroom doorway. She had no idea how long, just that he looked at her with loving eyes, like the way he'd always looked at their daughter, except with her there was this sexy blink that always happened when he was trying to see inside her. Like now.

"Don't."

"You mean I can't look at my beautiful wife?" he offered.

"Not now. I'm not much to look at."

"I wouldn't say that." He breathed next to her and wrapped his arms around her waist. She watched him from the large mirror. "I think we make a terrific couple," he said.

"Without a child," she added.

The smile faded. "Let's go to dinner."

***

"I don't think it's supposed to be easy," he said.

She smiled, this time for real. He'd brought her to a pizzeria. The place was decked out in red and white checkered tablecloths, waiters that looked as if their smiles were painted on, and plenty of water in clear, plastic pitchers.

"Welcome to The Pizzeria," the waiter touted.

Virginia blinked over at him. The boy was in white except for the green apron he had tied around his neck and waist. He was a tall boy, and sported gangly arms and some fine chin hairs - probably his first.

"Do you have Canadian bacon and pineapple?" she asked.

The boy moved his narrow hips back and forth in a Hawaiian sway. "Of course," he said, and Virginia held her tongue. It wouldn't have been polite to tease the boy, especially if he thought he was truly funny.

"We'll get a medium Canadian bacon as well as a pepperoni with extra cheese."

"Right. And to drink?"

Richard looked over at Virginia. He winked. "What would you like?"

"Just grab me a Coke and some water, please."

"Ditto for me."

"Anything else?" The boy swayed in the nonexistent wind, his narrow hips moving back and forth in the same Hawaiian dance.

"That should do it."

"Except when dessert comes. You'll not want to miss our cookies and cream."

"What's that?" Virginia asked.

The boy blinked over at her. "A large, warmed chocolate chip cookie with a scoop of vanilla ice-cream on top."

Virginia was suddenly hungry. "I think I'll have that first," she said.

Richard laughed. "Me, too," he said, his eyes watching the waiter as he left the table.

"So what do you think?" she asked.

"About what?"

"That kid?"

Richard brushed back his hair. It had grown longer since Beatrice's death, and she wondered why he hadn't cut it yet. Soon his hair would be long enough to put into a ponytail.

"Seemed kind of strange to me. Did you notice the hips swaying?"

"Couldn't miss it."

Richard took a sip of Coke. The water and Coke had been delivered moments before and Virginia had already downed half of her glass.

"So, what do you want to do this weekend?" Richard asked. At the first of the week they'd discussed going to the cemetery where Beatrice was buried, but Virginia had said she wasn't sure she was ready for that yet. He'd suggested the park. Didn't she love the swings, and wasn't it always her idea to take a load off by sitting amongst the trees? "What about the mountains?"

"Too cold, besides..." she smirked wearily at him, "you'll probably propose to me again."

He held up his right hand, palm forward. "Will not. I don't want to be turned down."

She forced a smile. "You know, maybe we should go to the mountains. There are good memories there. I can pack all the food you like and we can sit amongst the snow drifts like we used to."

"You really mean it?"

"Sure, why not."

***

It was with some reluctance that Virginia packed the food and prepared for their trip. She'd had a few days to think about the cold as well as the walk and wondered how she might convince Richard to do something else. What she really wanted to do was sleep. And eat. And sleep. And maybe he could hold her in the darkness.

"Ready?" he asked. Richard was standing at the kitchen doorway this time, and all she could think about was God standing in Paul's kitchen before Paul had died. How he'd smiled at her, how he'd prepared all of those doughnuts..."Virginia?"

"Sorry, honey. I was just thinking about God."

"Oh?" He gave her a little smile.

"It's not what you think."

"What?"

"About God. I was just remembering him in Paul's kitchen."

"I bet you miss him."

"Paul or God?"

It was a wicked question, but it made Virginia think about her friend and about God. Her friend because he'd practically died in her arms, and God, because he'd died for her, so very, very long ago.

The Change

"Richard?" She banged on the door to the bathroom but there was no response. The shower had stopped at least 10 minutes prior to her banging and now the room was silent. No shaving. No toilet flush. Nothing. "Richard!" She tried the door. It was locked.

Leaning her head against the door she couldn't hear a thing, but he had to be in there. Their non-existent hike up the mountains for a picnic replayed itself in her mind.

"You don't want to go? I thought..."

"I've changed my mind."

"Figures."

"I'm sorry, I just can't help myself."

He'd looked at her strangely and brushed passed her.

Her mind returned to the present. "Richard!"

"What?" he hollered.

"Oh, good. I was worried."

"About what?"

"You, silly." He was silent. "What are you doing?" she asked.

"Nothing. I'll be out in a second."

She waited at the door. A few minutes later the door opened. Richard's eyes were as red as her satin pajamas. She thought briefly of the baboon. "Are you okay?" she asked, touching him on the arm and feeling his skin. He hadn't yet put his shirt on.

"No. You?"

She watched him walk to the bedroom, reach inside the closet for one of his blue dress shirts, and put it on. He turned to her. "I don't think I'm going to go to work today," he said.

She laughed. "So why the dress shirt?"

He picked at it strangely. "I don't know. I guess I'm just used to wearing it. Can you go in my place?"

"You can't be serious."

"You used to work," he said. "I need a day off."

"Oh."

"Is that all you have to say?"

"Well, I suppose I can go. What will you do?"

He looked down at the floor. "I don't know, probably the stuff you've been doing lately."

"What's that supposed to mean?"

"Nothing."

She frowned over at him. "Well, okay, I'll go to work, open the shop. Is there anything specific you'd like me to do?"

He shrugged. "Oh, I don't know, sell some stuff."

***

The Gift – A Parable of the Key

It was the strangest thing she'd ever done. Work at *Just Desserts* without him. But it was sort of freeing, too, like standing on a mountaintop with a kite. There was no one hovering over her, no one to ask how she was doing, no one to wonder if she was going to make it through the day.

She opened the blinds, checked the register, and busied herself in the back room. There were a few spaces to fill in the front displays, and the *sale* sign, tucked in one of the small paned windows, had to be removed. The sale had obviously ended last week.

It was 9 a.m. She unlocked the door and invited the small group of waiting people inside.

A girl peered over at her. She was with her mother. "Joy?" she asked.

At least a year had gone by since she'd seen the girl, and she had grown taller, but still wore clothes much too large for her. Today it was a green dress with some sort of stain on the collar, though Virginia had to admit that the green emphasized her eyes.

"What will you have today?" Virginia asked.

The mother peered inside the display case. Her hair was a matted wad of black. Her eyes looked tired, and her smile was invisible. "She always wants the pink ones."

Virginia reached inside.

"With a ring on it," the woman, added blandly.

Virginia searched. "Looks like we're completely out of rings," she said.

19

"Figures." The woman looked over at her daughter. She and Richard had been married almost seven years, so the girl was at least 16. Joy had caught up with her mother some in height. She touched her mother's arm and smiled over at Virginia. "That's okay. One of the plain ones is fine," she said.

Virginia reached for a pink frosted cupcake. "Do you want it in a box?" she asked. "There is plenty of seating, if you'd like to eat here," she added, hoping that the two would stay for awhile longer. She wanted to take in the sweet growth of the girl, and remember everything, including how God had been a part of their first meeting when she was only ten. But it wasn't to be.

"Just put it in one of those white boxes like your husband does," the mother said.

Virginia reached for a box and placed the cupcake inside. "On the house," she said, though the mother had reached her hand inside her raggedy coat pocket.

"I always pay," grumbled the woman. "And I will pay now."

The change was splattered on the glass counter. With dirty fingernails the woman counted out the money. "That should do it," she said, and grabbing the box, handed it to her silent daughter.

"Thanks, Mom."

"Is there anything else I can get you?" Virginia asked.

"Some sanity," the woman answered.

Virginia watched Joy's eyes as they looked into hers. She tried to read the volumes of pain stored there. But the girl said nothing. "Thank you," she offered.

***

The smell of spruce filled the room. The soap Richard always used turned her mind for a moment to other things...He was sitting on the red couch watching some movie. "So, how was your day?" he asked, dipping his hand into a bowl of popcorn.

"Good. Yours?"

"Fine, as you can see."

Virginia took off her coat and hung it in the closet. She walked down the hall to remove her shoes. Passing Beatrice's bedroom, she stopped. "Richard!" she yelled, looking into the emptiness. "Where's all of the furniture?"

"Away, in the basement!" he hollered back, "and I've boxed the clothing and stuff and put it down there, too."

"All of it?" Suddenly Richard was standing there, his right arm carrying the popcorn bowl, his left hand dipping to retrieve yet another handful.

"All of it. I hope you don't mind."

"Mind? Of course I mind!" The words sprang from her aching throat, like an anxious cat. How could he do it? How could he clean up the room as if Beatrice had never been there?

Richard shrugged. "It was time, and I knew you wouldn't be cleaning it up anytime..."

"And that's as it should be. I respect her memory!"

"Then go to her graveside, don't keep all of this junk in the room, hoping that she'll return!"

"So that's it. You think I believe she'll come back!"

"Well, what else could it be?"

"I...don't know..." Her heart ached. She wanted to scream, but nothing came. For the next two hours Virginia sat in the lavender room and wept. Richard did not join her.

***

The following day Virginia returned to work. Richard had not spoken to her since the incident in Beatrice's room and she hadn't volunteered anything.

It was just two weeks before Christmas.

She wasn't sure why she hadn't thought to ask Richard about a tree. She'd wondered about gift giving this year, but hadn't even considered buying anything. Perhaps that wasn't right. Perhaps Beatrice would want them to celebrate the holiday. She would discuss it with Richard when she returned home.

But he was asleep after her day at the bakery and she hadn't wanted to wake him, so she'd pulled the *listening* stone from off of the mantel instead and held it within her hands. She stood gazing at the stones lined up on the mantel and realized how much she needed them now.

"So, you've come at last," she felt the stone of *listening*, say.

"Yes, God."

"And you're angry with me."

22

"Yes." She gulped and took the rock into the bedroom.

"You must trust me," he said.

"I know, but I miss her..."

"I know. She is well and happy."

"I'm glad."

"Trust that I know what's best. Think about your many blessings. You do have them, you know."

"You've read my mind," she said, "as usual."

"So trust that I know what's best for you."

She wiped at her eyes and dropped the rock of listening in her right coat pocket, just so she could remember it in the morning before work. She reached for the Bible.

She wasn't sure what was happening within the mind of her husband, but she also wasn't sure what to do next. Another week went by, and they spoke little; just short conversations at dinner (when they had them) and moments in the morning before she returned to work.

Richard had said nothing about her sacrifice, but then again, the house was clean when she returned home and the household chores seemed to be getting done, so she tried not to worry.

Tried was the key phrase.

Though she journeyed to *Just Desserts*, and her presence in the little bakery for the day soothed her mind and cleared her head, her return home would gather in the stress and make her feel as if her day away from home was not really worth the effort.

Still, she went. It was all she could do.

A week before Christmas she went out shopping for a Christmas tree without him and found a straggly one lying against the fence. It had been marked down to half price. She dragged the tree to the lot attendant, and in the freezing cold, paid for it. The man, who had a striking resemblance to God in the fisherman's cap, loaded the tree on top of her car, tying it down for her. She thanked him and drove home.

The driveway had already been cleared by her husband. That, and something was cooking on the stove when she dragged the tree in. He looked at her in amazement. "Pine needles are going to go everywhere," he said, and she had to smile. Hadn't that *once upon a time* been her line?

But she continued to drag the thing in as he watched, found the stand in the basement, and got busy trying to saw the bottom off the tree with the old hand saw. That's when he reached for her. "Let me help you," he said. "The least I can do is to help you saw the piece off."

The grinding of saw on wood came next, followed by a spattering clunk as the piece broke off. She reached for the broken trunk and stood. "Now put it in the tree stand. I'll get some water."

He smirked over at her and stood the tree up. Truly it was an awful, naked thing, but it was the best they could get this late in the season. She poured the water. "I've got to get the lights."

"No worries." He sat on the floor by the tree and looked up. She paused only once at the top of the stairs, taking him in, feeling the rock of *listening,* now in her pant pocket. Then, flicking on the light, she returned to the basement.

Life Patterns

The girl was wise beyond her years. "I might be able to help you with that," she said. Her mother looked sick, her skin yellow; she sat on the only vacant chair left in *Just Desserts*, her eyes staring into nothing, or so it seemed to Virginia. "We had a tree once."

"You don't have a tree?"

"Would be hard to cart around," said the girl, "since we're homeless."

"You're homeless?"

Joy yanked on her dirty shirt. It was orange and had small holes near the hem. Her short jeans barely touched her ankles. She wore dirty, black shoes. No socks.

"So what did you think, that mom and me, we were some stylish rock band?"

Virginia laughed. "Sorry," she said. "I had no..."

"Christmas was great for me once," she returned, avoiding Virginia's eyes. She breathed into the air as if somehow, even in this warm space, she could still see it, her breath flowing in and out like a thousand fluttering angels. "When dad was with us, and before mom..." She looked behind her to see her mother's head on the table. "Sorry."

She wasn't the only person who was sorry. Strange looks occupied the eyes of the visitors already eating or drinking. Before long, they'd be finding excuses to leave before they'd even have to, and Virginia wasn't even sure if she cared. She touched the stone of *trust* in her apron pocket and thought of how renewed she'd felt...renewed, since returning to her study of the Bible. Her daughter was gone, but, perhaps, it would be alright if she read about God.

"A pink one, please?" Joy asked, breaking Virginia away from her thoughts.

"Of course." She reached inside the case. Recently purchased, the glittering ring yet captivated the green eyes of her young friend. "Maybe one day I'll get married," she said.

So that was it.

"I'm sure you will," Virginia offered, placing the pink cupcake inside the small box, closing the sides, and handing the gift over the counter.

"Thank you." She turned, and nudging her mother, reached for the front door. Her mother looked up.

"What do you want?" she moaned.

"I have the cupcake, let's go."

Her mother stood. Every eye was on her, but the woman, stooped over like she was eighty, reached for her daughter's shoulder. "Help me up," she said.

The girl reached out a slender hand, and with the pink cupcake held within her right, led her mother out the door.

***

Richard didn't look well. Besides the redness of his nose and eyes, he looked as if all energy had been drained from his body. Lying in the bed, his head propped up with his pillow as well as hers, Virginia tried not to think about all of the unseen germs crawling around on it.

Instead she smiled over at him. "Had a hard day?" she asked.

"Sure."

"Eaten?"

"No."

"How long?"

"I don't know."

"Want something?"

He turned from her. "Just sleep. Maybe later."

The room smelled like a mixture of cough medicine and liquor. But Richard didn't drink and she couldn't see any bottles. Plenty of tissues had been strewn around and plenty of cough drops, so maybe that was it. Richard had a cold.

Moments later, as she sat in the chair opposite the bed watching him sleep, she remembered their life together, with and without Beatrice. She touched the stone of *trust*, now within the palm of her hand. It was no longer black, but the gray mists within it only reminded her of where she was spiritually - where she was without him. While Richard appeared to be wallowing in his loneliness, she wasn't doing much better away from him.

***

It was Christmas.

They sat near the tree and she was stunned at the beauty of it. No gifts this year. Nothing but bright lights, sparkling ornaments, and a tree that reflected where they were together. She, beginning to fill with light, he, still sorrowful, still remote. A thin, naked tree, just waiting...for what? She hadn't been able to find him, even now.

"So what should we do first?" he asked.

"I made plum pudding," she offered. "Don't you smell it?"

He sniffed, but his cold was hanging on like a pearl in an oyster shell not wanting to be found. If only they could find that oyster. If only...

"Wow. I think I smell it."

She stood, releasing his hand, and walked to the kitchen. Smells of cinnamon, nutmeg, and cloves filled her nostrils like a dream. It was ready.

***

She wasn't sure when the idea had come to her, maybe in the moment between sleep and that first moment when her eyes opened, but there it was. If nothing else the girl would have a little money to take care of her mother, and in working at *Just Desserts*, Joy would develop some well-needed confidence.

28

But Richard didn't agree. "You can't hire a homeless girl to work in the bakery," he said. It was morning, and the sky, a pale blue, a striking contrast to the workings of her heart.

"Why not? They need the money."

"Then donate something."

"That's not the same."

Richard stretched on the bed, begging her to return to it, but she was already at the window.

"I guess you're worried about the customers, all of the gawking customers..." Virginia said.

"I guess you could say that." He sat up and adjusted his pillow. He was no longer using hers, and she had since washed the pillow case.

"But I need to do something."

"Why?" he asked.

"I just feel it in my gut." She'd since forgiven him of the lavender room fiasco, and his cold had healed up nicely, but he was still spending much of his time at home and she, within the walls of *Just Desserts*.

"Well, your gut should tell you that you can't hire a girl just because you think she needs the money." He stood from the bed, and in the same moment, reached for her, pulling her into his arms. "You've changed," he said.

"I know." She brushed her cheek lightly against his. "We need some warmth here."

He kissed her neck, the first ounce of love he'd expressed in some time. She allowed it to continue, the soft yet prickly sensation of lips and chin traveling against her skin, making her smile. And then she thought of Joy.

***

Nearly two months later, Joy came in with her mother. It was February, and the chill of the air made Virginia want to curl into a small ball and sip hot chocolate for the entire day, though she realized a sedentary life was a pipedream, and not a very healthy one.

Someone had to work.

Richard kept house, and fairly nicely too, but Virginia just couldn't connect with him, at least where moving forward in life was concerned.

But she had the bakery. And she had Joy.

"So how are you today?" she asked Virginia.

"Very well," Virginia answered, reaching for a pink cupcake. Joy stood next her, an old coat draping her tiny frame. She wore the same black shoes without socks.

Weeks prior, she and Richard had gathered in the winter clothing. Two hats, two pairs of red gloves, a couple of scarves, socks, new coats and boots. They sat even now in the back room, and she hoped she'd managed the sizes correctly.

Walking into the back room, she returned with a medium-sized box in her arms. She sat it on the floor.

"What's this?" Joy asked, reaching to touch a hat that lay near the top.

"A hat," Virginia offered simply. "I also have a scarf for each of you, some gloves and..."

"We'll not be wanting charity," the mother said.

The Gift – A Parable of the Key

Virginia was stunned. Would she rather walk around cold?

"But Mom, this is good stuff," the girl said, lifting a hat and placing it on her head. It was perfect.

"We'll not be accepting charity." She reached for the woolen hat and pulled it off her daughter's head.

Virginia breathed slowly. Why was the woman so stubborn? Could she live in rags and refuse something that was offered freely? And then Virginia thought of God. God offered his gifts freely; in fact they were the very key to happiness, but sometimes she did not listen. Sometimes she didn't want the gifts. Sometimes, it just felt better to remain in her misery.

"The key to receiving these gifts might be of interest to you then," said Virginia. "I am positive you will take these gifts after what I tell you."

The woman blinked over at her and for the first time Virginia noticed her eyes, green like her daughter's. "What's your name?" she asked.

The woman hesitated. "Grace," she said, "but your husband knew that."

The comment had been said to prick her conscience, but Virginia was beyond the hurt. She just had to help them. "Grace," she repeated, looking into the woman's eyes. "I am in need of some help here. Dish washing, sweeping up, attending to the customers - baking. Are you and your daughter up for the task?"

The woman blanched. "You're kidding," she stammered, touching her coat and wiping her grimy hands against the worn fabric.

But Joy's eyes lit up like a Christmas tree. "Oh, Mom!" she sang, "it's an answer to our prayers!"

Fortunately, at that particular time, no other customers were at *Just Desserts*, but perhaps having other customers there to see what transpired that early February morning, would have been a life-changing experience, just as it was beginning to be a life-altering experience for Virginia.

Just Desserts

Maybe it was the way she told him, the sort of sly way she spoke about the new workers at *Just Desserts,* or maybe it was merely that she'd hired Grace and Joy *period* that had created such a frenzy within her husband's mind. Or maybe the frenzy had more to do with Virginia allowing the two to stay in the now vacant lavender bedroom.

"You what?"

"I've hired Grace and her daughter to work for us."

He stood up, the entire bowl of popcorn tumbling to the ground.

"Why would you do that?"

"Well, I told you...I said that I couldn't allow the daughter and her mother to be hungry anymore, and I couldn't allow them to be cold and without shelter, and so..."

"You didn't say any of that. You just...just wanted to hire them! Where are they now?" he asked hotly, reaching for the bowl.

There wasn't much time. "They'll be at the door in a second. I want you to be nice."

He scowled over at her. "Nice...nice? What do you think I am, some ogre?"

She winked at him.

"I can't believe you did this!"

"I hear them. Now, do as you promised." She smiled over at him but he didn't smile back.

***

"Hello, Virginia." The man in the fisherman's cap peered over at her from the opposite side of the counter. "How are you doing?"

Virginia grinned widely. She'd just shown Joy how to use the mixer for the latest batch of cupcakes, and her mother, Grace, was doing swimmingly. Virginia even wondered if the skill of baking had been part of her daily life before the woman and her daughter had left their home.

She realized there was a lot that she didn't know. Had Grace been married? Had they *ever* had a home? What had caused them to leave their previous life? And Richard? You could say that his heart was softening; albeit slowly. Their daughter's room had a new bed, two chairs and a table (so the girl and her mother could eat alone at times) and plenty of closet space for the clothing they were quickly earning.

At *Just Desserts*, while Grace worked, her daughter took some time away to read, but she was always eager to welcome customers with her winning smile. She was clean, beautiful, and charming, and no one seemed the wiser. For all they knew she was a new girl they'd hired, not the young girl who'd stood in rags months before, wanting a pink cupcake.

As for God, he was gazing at her, his eyes twinkling. "So what have you been up to?" he asked, peering down at the pink cupcakes once more filling the case.

"As if you didn't know."

He looked up at her again, this time more seriously. "Be careful," he began. "You are doing a good thing but it's important to be wise." She felt the stone of *optimism* in her apron pocket and smiled over at him.

Virginia's heart pounded. "What do you mean?" she asked, whispering this time, hoping Grace or Joy wouldn't see who she was talking with and that Joy would remain intent on her nature book.

"Just as I said," replied God. "Perhaps it's time to sit down with Grace and discuss her future plans."

Virginia tried to remain optimistic. Hadn't God once said that if she trusted him and listened to his voice, she would know what to do in her life; that she would know that it was by him that she was led? But of course. She was hearing him now, and he was telling her to be careful.

She decided to listen. "What should I say?" she asked, fearful now that she might brooch the subject awkwardly, making Grace mad.

"That is entirely up to you," God answered, and Virginia felt somehow deflated. Why wouldn't God tell her what to do; it would be so much easier that way.

But God only smiled. "I would like one of those pink cupcakes," he said, waving his hand in their general direction.

"Boxed?" Virginia asked.

"No, just plate it," said God.

Virginia reached for the cupcake, and, carrying it to the back table, placed it on a small white plate. She turned and offered it to God. "On the house," she said, making God smile. He took the cupcake and plate and walked over to where Joy was sitting.

***

As the weeks went by, Virginia found herself getting more and more frustrated with her house-guests. The room, if you could call it that, was such a mess she wondered if they'd soon be harboring other guests.

Mice had never been welcome in her home, whether they'd been purchased or otherwise, and she was not about to welcome them now.

Still, for days on end, the door would be shut - the two doing *who knows what*, and some of the meals she offered had been met with distance. "Wouldn't it be better if we had our meals alone?" Joy's mother would ask at least three times a week, though she'd never offered to cook one of them herself.

Both mother and daughter did better at work, but if the truth be known, it was the daughter, not the mother, who had a knack for baking and almost everything else in the kitchen. Just recently, her mother had even feigned sickness and had stayed in her home while everyone else worked.

The situation made Virginia crazy. What was the woman doing while they were away? Would she even have a home to return to?

At night she'd whine at her husband, only to be met by steely eyes. She knew what he was thinking; more important she knew what she had done.

One day she couldn't take it any longer. The two had spent the evening alone, as usual, and when the door finally opened, a smell like death reeked from the very walls of the lavender room.

"What have you been doing in here?" Virginia shouted at her guests, as her husband looked on. She peered inside only to be shoved back. The place was a terror.

"So you don't trust me!" Grace wailed.

"No, I don't! Look at this mess! Do you believe in cleaning - at all?"

The woman blinked at her. She didn't look right. No, her eyes didn't look right.

Joy peered behind her mother like a small child. But she wasn't a small child. What was the woman doing to her only daughter? Whatever it was, she wouldn't stand for it.

"We have a right to our privacy!" the woman screamed, taking her daughter by the hair and pulling her in front of her.

"I'm so..." Joy began.

"Don't you go apologizing!"

"We're... in... their...house," Joy stammered.

Grace glared at Virginia. "It doesn't matter," she wheezed, letting go of her daughter's hair and taking her daughter by the hand. "I suppose you want us to leave."

Virginia was dumb struck. What could she possibly say to this woman? Do? And then the words came:

"We will not allow drugs in this house! I don't care if it's booze or needles!"

Joy blinked her large green eyes. "I told you, I told you they'd find out!"

Grace scowled. "I told *you* to be quiet."

Joy laughed. But it was a sickly laugh, almost as if she couldn't believe what her mother had told her to do.

"Look. We really appreciate the place, but we have to get along in this life the same as you," Grace said, pulling at her daughter's arm, and, at the same time, trying to get around Virginia and Richard.

"What about our things?" Joy asked, peering behind her.

"Oh, yeah. We'll just get our things, and then we'll be out of your way."

"Sounds good to me." Even as she said the words Virginia knew that part of what she'd just said was a lie. What was good was having the mother vanish from off the planet. Perhaps there was still time to save the daughter.

"Excuse us," Joy said, following her mother into the lavender room.

Richard blinked over at her. "I'm sorry," he said, taking Virginia's hand. "We should have done this weeks ago. This is our house, we should feel safe."

They left the two to pack up. At the end of the hall they waited. Moments later Joy and her mother rejoined them. But something wasn't right.

It was a feeling more than anything else, an aching feeling of loneliness that suddenly enveloped Virginia's heart. How could she do it? How could she let Joy go? She was...she was...And then the words were there, as if they'd always existed, and only needed the right moment for release.

"Don't go. I...I mean we'll get it to work out."

Richard looked at her numbly, but said nothing.

Virginia touched Joy on the arm. Her skin was clean and her beautiful blond hair was brushed and styled. Everything from her head to her feet was shined up. No one would have ever known she'd once been homeless.

And then a new thought struck her, like a glowing wind, a breeze...

Changing the outside of both Grace and Joy was all that she and Richard had managed to do. Both mother and daughter were cleaner, surely, but after only a few weeks, their old life appeared to be seeping through their otherwise clean exterior. How could she have been so wrong? Merely changing the outside had not really changed how mother and daughter thought about life.

Virginia thought about cupcake making, about her focus on making the experience for Joy and Grace a positive one, and she'd seen some changes in behavior, an inner light surely; and yet, were mother and daughter still anchored to the life they'd been living for how-many-years now?

Yes, it was God who'd come into the bakery and told her that trouble was coming, but what had he said exactly? What was it that she'd been counseled to do?

"Perhaps it's time to sit down with Grace and discuss her future plans," God had said. But how could she do that, now that mother and daughter were leaving?

"I bet you have dreams," prompted Virginia, thinking of God's words.

Grace was already outside. As the girl stood waiting, a tear dripped down her left cheek. "I did once," she said, turning from Virginia.

A small breeze like breath, blew in through the door of their three bedroom home.

"Maybe if we sat down and talked about it," she offered.

But the girl only continued to cry. "Thank you for the nice meals, and the clothes, and this...this beautiful home, but I have to go."

Virginia looked out at the snow. She felt the bitter air against her cheeks. It would be a month or two yet before the weather warmed up. She nodded at the girl and watched her go, for the words would no longer come.

***

They hadn't eaten dinner; in fact, the entire evening had been spent trying to figure out ways to get them back. With the entire list in front of her, from taking a walk and dragging them back, to finding another home and paying for them to live in it, what kept coming back to Virginia's mind was how the inside of both Joy and her mother, had not yet caught up with the outside.

Could new clothes, a daily shower, and plenty of food change what had been growing in both of their hearts for years? And what about the inside? What desolation and bad habits held mother and daughter captive? What would finally release them both?

A sudden light entered Virginia's own heart. What had God said about making the inside of the cup clean *first*? She'd read about it, probably not recently, but the thought of cleaning the inside of the cup before the outside revealed itself again and made her walk to the bookshelf for the Bible. She reached for the black Bible with the gold lettering and returning to her husband, read: "Woe unto you...for ye make clean the outside of the cup and of the platter, but within [you] are full of extortion and excess. Thou blind...cleanse first that which is within the cup and platter, that the outside of them may be clean also" (Matthew 23:25-26, KJV).

She placed the book on the table. "So what do you think?" she asked.

Richard smiled and touched her hair. "I think," he said, smiling widely, "that perhaps we have been doing it all wrong."

He'd said *we*, but she knew what he meant and his words were the last thing she needed. "Okay, so I'm human," she offered. "String me up."

"Anywhere?" he asked.

"Anywhere, what?"

"Strung up." He laughed.

"I'm serious."

"So am I."

"I mean, about the cup. Do you think we need to take them to church?"

"What?" He laughed again, but this time it sounded more like a choke.

"I'm serious. It's been a long time since *we've* been to church."

"We've *never* been to church," Richard offered.

"Yes, but..."

He touched her hair again and looked easily into her eyes. "I think..." he said, "that it's time for dinner. Do you want to cook or shall I?"

***

It was late winter before Virginia saw Joy again. This time she was without her mother. "I bet you thought you'd never see me again," she said.

Virginia nodded, remembering the angry words, the separation that had been caused by the drugs and alcohol in the lavender room.

The girl pressed her grimy hands against the glass countertop and looked in. "I don't know what it is about those pink cupcakes, but they make me feel better...somehow..."

"Want one?"

The girl held her hand up. Dark lines of dirt followed the lines of her fragile palm. Somehow, she looked even smaller than when she'd last seen her.

Virginia noticed the coat she had given her and the gloves and hat, but the colors had changed; they appeared as muted and withdrawn as the girl wearing them.

"I don't have any money," Joy said, raising her face to Virginia. Her eyes looked tired. "But I didn't come to mooch off of you anyway," the girl continued. "I was hoping you had a job for me."

"Of course..."

"Mother is dead."

Virginia's heart stopped. She looked past the girl. Two tables were already filled, and along with them, inquisitive eyes.

"Mother...drugs...I told her not to take them but..."

"Where is she?"

"Who knows? She wasn't at the shelter, under the freeway, at the park, nowhere..."

"So you came here?"

The girl's eyes swam with tears. "Does that surprise you? What would they have done with me, huh?" She wiped her eyes. The tears had started with the telling of her mother's death, and now, the dirt was mixed in and the girl's eyes appeared irritated.

"How old are you now?"

"Funny you should ask," Joy said. "I just had a birthday. I think I'm seventeen." The girl smiled but it was about as long-lasting as a hiccup. "I wanted to come in, get a cupcake, steal a candle, you know, sing. But Mother would have none of that. Told me that you'd force us to come back. But I wanted to come back..."

"You did?" She touched the girl's hands then, still planted on her glass counter. But the girl didn't jump and she didn't move her hands. Slowly, Virginia curved her hands around her slim ones. What could she possibly say?

She looked over at the customers. One of the group, a girl and her boyfriend were getting up; the second, a family of four, continued to peer over at her as if waiting for what she might do next. But she had no idea what to do, no idea at all.

"I'm sorry," Joy finally offered, and Virginia smiled.

"I'm sorry, too. I'm sorry about your mother." She released the girl's hands and continued to the front of the counter. "What would you say to a home-cooked meal tonight?"

Joy's eyes lit up. "Food?"

She heard some negative talk in the corner but ignored it.

"What's your favorite?"

"Favorite?"

But the girl had probably not eaten in days and suddenly Virginia felt particularly stupid. Joy wouldn't care about a favorite food, she would just like to eat. But the girl's next words surprised her: "I like fish," she said.

***

Richard took a bite of fish stick. So, it wasn't the fish Virginia had first considered when Joy had told them what she wanted for dinner, but in a somewhat roundabout way, it still was fish.

She laughed to herself.

Joy had washed her hair and she smelled as fresh and clean as a newborn babe. New clothing, clothing that Virginia had saved for the few months after she and her mother had left them, still fit the young girl, albeit loosely around her arms and legs. Joy was growing up, but she still appeared smaller than the average 17-year-old.

"These are good," she said. "I never liked salad though, but now, it doesn't really matter what I eat."

Richard blushed. "I'm glad you'll eat it," he said. "You can't eat fish sticks all of your life."

The girl blinked. They sat around a square table and Joy's face was to the window. Virginia and her husband sat on either side of the table, their typical places.

"Thank you for the rolls," Joy said, adding butter. "We always had rolls at dinner. I remember once when my dad started choking on one," she began, chewing on the roll in between portions of the story. "He was choking and my mom got up and slammed him on the back, trying to dislodge it, you know..." She looked up. Virginia was silent, so was Richard. There was no way on God's green earth that she was going to say anything...now.

"Well, father yelled, so the thing had been dislodged. After that, Mother never made rolls." The girl grew silent. "So it's nice to have them now."

Virginia wasn't sure what to say. What a strange story, and what, truly, had she gotten herself into?

When the meal ended, Joy helped her gather and rinse the dishes so that she could put them in the dishwasher, all the while whistling some tune that Virginia didn't know. Once finished, they gathered in the living room to have a chat.

It was awkward at first - sort of the feeling you get when going into a job interview, or meeting with God, but Virginia knew one thing; if she and Richard were going to take the girl in, they would have to know something about her past. They would have to do this legally, and if that meant some prying was called for, then so be it.

Having been told that Grace was dead, and no way to find out who the girl really was, it was the only thing they could do anyway. So while the girl sat, playing with the white tassel on the pillow nearest her, Richard and Virginia looked at each other, hoping that the other one would begin first.

The silence got to Richard. "So, have you been to school?" he asked.

Joy smiled wearily. "Used to," she said, "before mother pulled me out."

"How old were you?"

"Eight." The girl peered over at him from behind the pillow. "What are all those rocks on your mantel for?" she asked.

Virginia's heart stopped. "We'll talk about that later," she said hastily.

"What school did you attend?"

The girl hesitated. "Kennedy." She stood, taking the pillow with her, and found her way to the mantel. "These are pretty cool," she said. "Can I have one?" With a deftness only a teen could manage, the stone of trust was quickly swept into her hand. "It's smooth," she said, her eyes opening wide. "Hey, it's changing color!"

Virginia's greatest fears realized, she stood from the couch. "Hand me the stone," she said, holding her hand out.

But the girl only peered into the cup of her hand. "Really!" she sang. "The stone is turning white!"

"Figures," Richard mumbled.

Virginia turned. "What's that supposed to mean?" she said, her heart pounding.

Joy suddenly released the stone into Virginia's hand. The stone, once white, had turned gray.

"That's cool. What do the other stones do?"

"Nothing," said Richard.

The girl sat. "This is one strange place," she said. "I mean, you guys are great and everything..." A sudden tear welled up in the girl's left eye. She brushed it with her hand. "I guess I just miss Mom. And I can't even visit her, you know? I have no idea where she's been buried."

Virginia didn't want to think about that. Where did they bury the homeless anyway? And had she even been found? If not, she didn't want to consider the condition of her body, or where she was lying.

"So where have you been living?" Virginia asked.

The girl hugged the pillow even tighter. "Oh, wherever we could. The park. Under bridges. In the winter we had to find our way to the shelter."

"Which one?"

"Safe Haven."

***

The girl was asleep in the lavender room; Virginia couldn't sleep.

"So?" Virginia asked.

"I don't think we should bring the girl there. I'll stop by tomorrow."

"But what about the store?"

"Take Joy with you tomorrow. I'll figure it out."

***

Richard returned but he wasn't smiling. "You'd think they'd be organized, what with all of the transients and such in that crusty building." Richard was as white as a sheet. Evidently his trip to *Safe Haven* hadn't gone well.

"Did you find her?"

"In a manner of speaking, yes." He reached for a cupcake. Joy was looking through a teen magazine and chewing slowly on a cupcake.

"Keep your voice down. Let's go in here." The room that housed their cooking and baking supplies was about as organized as their garage, and that wasn't saying much. Maybe she could get Joy to help her straighten it up a bit.

Richard ran a hand through his hair. "She had no ID on her, but after checking around the local shelters her body was discovered in an alley by the freeway. Looks like she had no family other than her daughter. Her husband is nowhere to be found. He could be alive or dead, they don't know."

"What of other relatives?"

Richard shrugged. "It's sad, I know. But I guess the good news is that she doesn't have to legally be shipped off to some crazy uncle." He picked up a bowl with pink frosting and plunged a finger into it.

"Richard!"

"Sorry." He sat the bowl down and licked the pink icing off of his finger. "But it was so weird. I felt as if I was the criminal, as if I had killed that woman. They wanted to know where the daughter was now. I lied. I told them I didn't know."

"Joy was already in the missing person's file," he continued, looking straight into Virginia's eyes. "They seemed quite excited to see me. I've got a bill for the burial costs." He handed her a white sheet of paper. "Evidently, any way the city can be relieved of this financial expense, is a burden off their backs."

Virginia looked down at the paper. The bill was paid in full, a mere $695 for cremation services.

"Oh, Richard. Cremation?"

"It's the cheapest route when relatives can't be found."

"Yeah, but..."

"They couldn't find Joy, and there was no other living relatives that they knew about; the county took the cheapest route, though I was told she had a brief funeral supplied by the coroners."

"So where are the ashes?"

"At the downtown cemetery. They've put her remains in the garden mausoleum there."

"That's only a few minutes' drive. Maybe we should take Joy..."

"It might be better if we don't..."

"Why?"

"There's no marker with her name; basically, she's buried with the others. They told me that the county doesn't pay for the extra expense of an individual marker. Just a number. She's 34."

Virginia didn't know what to think. But Joy had to know where her mother was, didn't she? She watched her from a short distance just finishing off of the pink cupcake. "We need to tell her anyway," she said. "The girl needs to know."

***

Telling Joy about her mother wasn't Virginia's only worry. As she made her way through the day, making cupcakes, doughnuts, and whatever else needed to be done, she thought about the secret. They harbored a homeless teen.

She knew in some states this was breaking the law.

But what choice did she have?

The girl needed them, and they couldn't put her back in a shelter. She and Richard knew her as 'best' as they could, not really knowing her. She hadn't told them much, and Richard had received few of Grace's 'valuables' even though he had footed the bill for her cremation; "We knew the mother and daughter," he'd offered.

"So my mother is really gone?" she asked. The girl had changed into another outfit - her third for

50

the day. She was wearing her favorite color - red, and the stripes across her belly and chest reminded Virginia of something in nature, although she couldn't quite place what it was.

"She's gone." Richard touched her hand but she didn't react. "But you have this."

With a gentle hand Richard reached for the necklace in his shirt pocket, a necklace Virginia hadn't even seen, until now. It was a simple thing, a small, ornately carved key, half the size of her index finger, hung on a silver chain; but it made the girl smile. A tear ran down her cheek until she brushed it away. With a dainty hand she reached for it, and then, asking for assistance, had Richard place the chain around her neck. It fell just below her collar bone.

She touched it. "Thank you," she said.

"They wanted you to have it," Richard said.

"They?"

"Those at *Safe Haven*."

"So you went."

Richard shrugged. Virginia looked deeply into Joy's face, but the girl didn't meet her gaze. She looked down at the key.

"Mother always loved this," she said. "Told me that it was the key to her heart and that one day it would be opened and I could see it."

Joy's mother must have been speaking metaphorically, but her daughter seemed to understand. So, she had the key to her mother's heart, a heart that had never really been opened. Or had it?

"You're probably wondering where I should go next?" Joy offered, touching the key and then looking at them both, alternately, like she was at court and they were two of those who had come to the trial, sitting way beyond the witness stand.

"We should probably take you back to the shelter."

"What?" She gaped at them, her green eyes large and searching.

"What we mean to say is," Virginia began, though the words tightened inside her throat, "perhaps you would like to go to a teen facility, or...something..."

"You don't like me, is that it?"

The girl's face had suddenly gone pale, almost as if the very thought of being alone again in a strange place was beyond her coping skills.

"That's not it." Richard's face was soft. He touched her hand again. This time she withdrew.

"My mom wanted me to be with you. She told me that if she ever left this earth I was to find you."

Richard and Virginia were silent. Actually, Virginia had thought about taking the girl in numerous times, and had discussed it with Richard.

"Would you like to live here?" Virginia asked.

"Oh, please!"

Richard coughed. "You would really like to live with us?" he asked. He didn't touch her this time but looked at her, as if trying to read all of the emotions the girl could not put into words.

Safe Haven

"I had a feeling you had her," the woman behind the counter said. "I mean, it was written all over your face."

"Why didn't you..."

The woman brushed a thick hand through her thinning black hair. "I guess I had a choice, and you seemed nice enough." She blinked over at Richard. "I hope my instincts were right." She reached below the counter and retrieved a cardboard box without a lid. "I've been saving this for you," she said.

Richard looked down. In the box was a red hat, some mittens, and a torn yellow notebook. No pen.

"How is Joy doing?" the woman asked.

"Fine," Richard answered. "But..."

"No worries. Are you considering foster care and possibly...adoption?"

Joy was at home with Virginia; it would have been difficult for the girl to return to a place filled with cockroaches or rats. To the naked eye, the family shelter that also served as a foster care and adoption facility, wasn't the worst he'd seen; the white paint looked fairly fresh, and the place was picked up, but one could never tell.

He looked behind her. A family of four stood behind her, though he really hadn't needed to look. The smell of dirt and sweat penetrated his nostrils and funneled its way through his skin. He tried not to cough.

"Isn't there a lot of paperwork?" he asked.

"Plenty." The woman smiled. "But worth it for a girl like Joy. You need to return her," she added lazily. "I mean, we need to know she is with you, and we really need to do this whole thing legally..."

"What do you know about her?"

"With her mother dead, she has no living relatives that I know of. Not even a father." She paused for a moment, and looked searchingly into his eyes. "Evidently, the girl and her mother have been on their own for about eight years. Before that, Joy's father was in the picture. His death brought some pain to Joy's mother. But I've said enough. Why don't I give you this?" The woman reached for a piece of paper. "Then I can take care of these folks, here. You don't mind, do you?"

Richard turned briefly. "No of course not," he said, smiling at the couple.

With the paper and yellow notebook before him, he briefly scanned the "First Contact" paper. The form was written in basic 'check the correct box' answer format asking for his particular interest in *Safe Haven*, how he'd heard about it, and included blanks for his name, address, phone number, and email address. He quickly filled out the form and returned it to the woman at the front desk who smiled at him.

"Good. Let's set up your orientation. Can you meet next week, say Wednesday, at 9?"

Richard had no idea. He'd have to talk to Virginia. "Can I call you?" he asked.

The woman blinked. "Sure, but Joy needs to be here by tomorrow morning."

Richard touched the yellow notebook now under his left arm. Why had the woman given him such a prize when she had no clue who he was? And the key? Why give him these items if he was not legally entitled to them?

Once inside the car he sat behind the wheel, took a deep breath, and looked down at the yellow front cover. It revealed a cover page with stark black letters that read:

Property of: Grace Sorenson,
mother of Joy Sorenson,
in search of a better life this day,
February 1.

***

Joy scowled up at the woman. "Why can't I live with Virginia and Richard?" she asked.

Richard took her arm. Fortunately, all of the beginning paperwork had been filled out; unfortunately, there was still some red tape before he could actually bring her home.

"It's what my mother wanted," Joy added.

"We know that."

Joy smiled over at Richard. "You haven't read all of my mother's book yet," she said. "It's in there."

So that was it.

"You'll see your new parents on Wednesday. You remember this place..." the social worker began.

"Sure."

"We'll take care of you until then."

"And then I can go home?"

"Not quite. There is some training for your new parents, a home study..."

Joy rolled her large green eyes. "I'll be 18 by the time you figure this stuff out! Legal and on my own!"

"When is your birthday?"

"December 24."

"Oh, yes, I remember now. The Christmas child."

"I am NOT a child," said Joy.

"Well, taking care of the paperwork, the classes, all of the..."

Joy leaned in. "You'd better do it quick. I don't think I can wait a year."

The woman smiled, and looked over at Richard. "Do you think you can manage it?" she asked.

"Leaving Joy, you mean?" he answered.

"No, taking care of her as a teenager."

Joy blinked, and squeezed his arm. "We'll see you soon," Richard said.

"I guess."

"And before too long we will be a true family."

***

"Listen to this:

'February 20. Went to the doctor today. Probably my last appointment. Living in a small apartment, but the money doesn't stretch as much as I want it to. Joy seems depressed. She is young and doesn't understand. It has taken me years to do this, and Joy need never know.'

That's the end of that entry. The next one starts:

'Joy is sick and the money is gone. I have just a few days to find the rent before March. I should have planned better...Jobs are scarce and I haven't held one in years. Even with all of the drinking there was still money somehow...but Tom is no longer with us...'"

Virginia paced the bedroom floor and it was all she could do to keep calm. "This sounds serious."

"It might be. Maybe we can read more later." Richard slid into bed and patted the sheet. "Why don't you come to bed? It's late."

Virginia looked at the clock. "Okay, so it's late, but I need to get this journal read."

"All in one night?" He smiled. "Besides, there are other things to do around here."

"Oh, is that so?" She shut the book and placed it on the nightstand before slipping into bed. The old routine had returned. Richard had returned, body and soul.

**

"I can't believe you're here!" The scream of Joy filled *Safe Haven* and eyes peered over at them briefly. "I mean, I thought I was going to die not seeing you two!" Joy plopped in the adjoining chair and stared at them. "You wouldn't believe the terrible...food." She turned to check her surroundings. "And the boys, all they want to do is try to kiss me."

"What?" The remark, though apparently sincere, had shocked Virginia. "Well, what are you going to do about it?"

"What boys?" Richard asked.

She peered behind her. "That one over there with the dark shirt and white hair. Don't you think he looks like an albino? And him-" She pointed her slim finger on the other side of the room. "He's short."

Richard coughed. "So, you like them, huh?" he asked.

"Like them? I'm trying to tell you..."

"Ah, Mr. and Mrs. Stone. Glad you could make it."

Virginia stumbled to her feet. A tall, stout woman in her 50's peered down at her. Richard stood. "Well, hello again," he said. They shook hands.

"The meeting will begin in a moment."

Virginia searched for a name badge. There was none. "So, who was that?" she asked, when the woman had retreated to the front of the room.

"The woman behind the counter. The one I've been working with."

"I suppose she has a name."

"I suppose you're right. Funny thing is, I've never heard it."

The Gift – A Parable of the Key

"It's Jean. Jean Rasmussen. She's not really the boss here, but she really likes to tell people what to do."

Richard smiled and took Joy by the arm. "And what, pray tell, have you been doing the last couple of days...besides, kissing boys?"

Joy blushed. "I told you," she whispered. "They tried to kiss me but I wouldn't let them. And besides, they have crummy books over here. I like yours better."

Virginia thought about Joy's love of nature and wished she'd thought to bring the book along. As it was, it was enough to remember to bring herself. She was so nervous she could hardly breathe.

After an initial introduction by a few of the teens living at the facility, they were sent away, and she and Richard had to listen without Joy. It was just as well. Virginia got to the point where she wanted to block out the worse case scenarios and just take in the good stuff.

Two lengthy speakers and many forms later, they were able to leave - without Joy.

***

Three weeks later, on a calm Sunday in March, Joy was gone from *Safe Haven*. And although it didn't take a rocket scientist to figure out why she'd gone, it was where she'd gone that worried Virginia and Richard the most.

"She is a great escape artist," said Jean. Her bulky form leaned against the counter as she spoke. "I guess I should have told you about that. But she...when she was with her mother, was always coming and going. Are you sure she's not at your place?"

"Why would we be here if she was?" Richard said. He looked angry.

"Right...Right. She took everything with her. Pillow, blanket, toiletries, and of course her coat and the other items you gave her. She practically slept with them. I'm so sorry..."

"How long has she been gone?" Virginia asked.

"Must have left last night. Learned of her escape this morning when her bed was empty."

"So, no one checks on these kids?"

"Well, sure. But...you must know that Joy has been in and out of shelters her entire life. If things aren't going her way..."

"What wasn't going her way?" Richard asked.

"Being here, without you two. It's practically all she talked about. Being in your home. Are you sure she isn't there?"

"We're sure," said Virginia. "So where do you think she went?"

"Wish I could tell you. She slept under viaducts sometimes, at other times in the park. But it's cold now, as you know; she would want to find some better shelter."

It occurred to Virginia in that moment that there was only one place she knew of, other than their home, that the girl would go. Or maybe two. But it wasn't until they'd left the facility that she felt free to tell Richard about either of them.

The Key

"That book of Grace's is more cryptic than Egyptian hieroglyphics," said Virginia, facing her husband. "But I think I know where the girl is."

"And that would be?"

"We need to start where her mother is buried, or entombed, or whatever you call it when a person is cremated. Or we can start at *Just Desserts*. She doesn't have a key to the place but that girl could probably break in if she wanted to; and not having an alarm on the premises would make it that much easier."

"Let's start there," said Richard. "If she isn't at the bakery, we'll work our way downtown."

***

Just Desserts was closed every Sunday - Virginia's idea - but they were both disappointed to find that Joy was not there. Not in the back room. Not sitting at one of the tables. Not hiding in a closet, though both Richard and Virginia doubted that a 17-year-old would do such a thing.

Still, they would be safe and look.

Without customers, the place breathed of vacancy and loneliness, and after fifteen minutes of looking, it was time to venture out.

The streets were clear, but it was early March. Bundling was still necessary, including hats, scarves, coats, boots, and often, thick tights for women. Virginia was glad of one thing: At least the roads weren't icy.

She prayed in that moment that Joy was warm, wherever she was, and that their journey to find her and bring her home was a short one.

But some dreams weren't meant to be realities.

At the cemetery, they looked for the spot, what Sunset Cemetery called, "Garden Abbey." Trudging through snow and past tombstones draped with lacy ice crystals, they finally found the spot on the northwest side. Here they stopped.

"This is interesting," said Virginia. She looked down to find a large slab of cement engraved with dates, but without names, lined up in rows like soldiers waiting for a command.

"What day did you say Grace died?" she asked.

"The coroner recorded it as December 28."

"Here it is. The last one." She pointed. The carving appeared fresh; the black engraving had not yet grayed like the others. She bent to touch it. The stone was cold.

The cloudy sky was darkening. Joy wasn't anywhere that she could see.

The Gift – A Parable of the Key

***

Back inside the car, Virginia rubbed her hands in front of the heater vent. Though gloved, they had still managed to absorb the chill. "So, what do you think?" she asked. "I mean, if Joy isn't here, where else would she go?"

Richard turned out of the parking spot and began to drive. "You said you knew of another place, I thought."

"Oh, that." Virginia was more than slightly embarrassed that the idea had even come to her at all. I mean, how would they know where to look? All she had was a memory of a key around Joy's slim neck, and that journal at home. Maybe it held a secret. She'd started the journal but hadn't finished it.

"Do you remember how excited Joy got when we gave her that key and chain?"

Richard smiled. "It was like the sun suddenly lit up in her eyes. Who could forget?"

Virginia's heart pumped. There was silence in the car, and although Virginia's body was warming, there was something disturbing about the silence between them, almost as if he knew something she didn't. Finally she asked, "Grace's journal - have you read all of it?"

He nodded.

"When?"

"When, what?"

"When did you read it?"

Richard colored. "That same night," he said, "when I got you into bed instead of allowing you to read it. I waited until you were asleep..."

"Why? I mean, why didn't you tell me?"

Richard's face softened. Now, it was a pleasing pink tone. "I'm sorry, honey. I was curious at first, but once I got reading I felt as if maybe I needed to think on what I'd read a bit before discussing it with you."

Virginia couldn't be angry. She felt the same way about the yellow journal; it should have been important to both of them. So what had her husband found? "Stop the car," she said, "there, over at that park. We need to talk."

The place was bare of people, and all of the leaves had drifted to the earth, where they'd glued themselves. He grinned over at her. "I can't remember the last time we *parked.*" He paused before continuing. "Virginia, before I say anything, you've got to promise me not to get angry."

"Okay, I promise. So?"

"Promise?"

She breathed in and out. "Okay! Enough already. Tell me."

"Grace was having an affair. Her husband found out. The drinking began."

"What?"

"I said..."

"I know what you said. But I thought the journal started after they'd left him, not before."

Richard turned to face her. His eyes looked sad and reflective. "The journal starts out with their first few months away from home. Grace talks about trying to find food to eat, a place to sleep, meeting you and me...and then, about midway through the book she shares some stuff...I wonder if Joy knew."

"Knew about what?" Her heart pounded.

"About the affair, about the abuse."

"What abuse?"

"When Joy's father got drunk, he also got violent."

"Oh." She was thoughtful for a moment trying to take it all in. "Well, Joy must have seen that. I can't imagine someone getting violent without a child knowing about it."

"That's what I thought."

"What else?"

"Well, there's the bit about the key."

Virginia nodded.

"Seems the key really does hold some special meaning. It was Grace's key. She got it from her mother after her death. Evidently, it was left to her."

"Wow."

"But that's not all. I guess the key opens an old box." Her husband reached for her hand. It had warmed some and she took it easily remembering the first time he'd looked at her this way and the second time he'd proposed. "I think Joy has gone to her old house. She has gone with the key to retrieve whatever is inside that old jewelry box."

***

Virginia stumbled to the bedroom and picked up the yellow notebook. Sure enough, on the back inside cover, was a thick piece of tape that must have been partially removed by her husband.

Joy, it read, *here is the key. The jewelry box is yours. The old man promised me he'd take very good care of it, though some secrets are best left buried. Let this key be a reminder, and remember my love for you. RWYA.*

"So it's buried. But that could be anywhere! And with an old man, no less! No name. Nothing. We don't even know where Joy and her mother lived; Joy never got that far in telling us. And we've received all of the paperwork. Everything."

"I know." Richard sat on the bed and patted a place for her beside him. "Look, that child is almost an adult and she's used to being out in the cold. She's old enough to get a job, and perhaps in time, get a place for herself. Maybe it's okay..."

"Okay? The child, as you say, is only 17! What were you doing at age 17? Surely not shopping around for a place to live!"

"No, but I was working, and you need to remember that Joy knows the streets..."

A dark thought entered Virginia's mind. Anything, but that.

He held her close. "We'll keep looking. And we'll look until we find her."

***

By April, Joy still hadn't returned to *Safe Haven.* And she hadn't shown up for a cupcake at *Just Desserts.* The paperwork, for a girl they would probably never see again, had halted. In its place were long nights of searching and reading, and days when Virginia could hardly focus on the task at hand. She and Richard grew closer in love and companionship than ever before, but life just wasn't the same without Joy.

Jean Rasmussen, the social worker, had almost given up hope that the girl would ever return. "It's to be expected," she'd said on their last visit in late March. "We lose many teens around her age, some even earlier. That's why foster care and eventual adoption are so important early on."

Virginia's face burned but she didn't say a word. If they'd been able to take Joy in early on, take care of her, even before the foster parenting stuff was finished, the girl wouldn't be gone.

Her body ached as she got into the car, and her anger couldn't be removed.

Once home, Richard placed an arm around her shoulders. "We'll find her, like I said." His breath smelled of recently chewed gum, his skin like Irish Spring.

"But how?"

"We just will." He smiled over at her and kissed her on the cheek.

The Journal

March 15.

Joy and I have found a safe place, actually it's more of a place for her than for me. There are times only a drink will satisfy me and besides, Joy deserves a nice, warm meal every once in awhile...

As she read, Virginia couldn't help but think about the woman and the terrible things she had done to her daughter. She was upset, and again wondered how much Joy knew about her mother. As she grew up surely she must have discovered her mother's journal at one time or another and read it when Grace was too overcome with the liquor to do anything but sleep. Then Virginia remembered the needles in the lavender room...

"It's amazing to me that Joy has lived as long as she has," she said, placing the journal on her lap.

Richard appeared reflective. His eyes traveled past her own and to somewhere far beyond them both. "I hope Joy isn't drinking," he said, "and taking drugs.

Do you think she stayed clean in order to help her mother?"

Virginia didn't know. She hoped so, but she continued to read:

March 21.

See the picture in the corner? Joy's own artwork. We found a fairly warm place in the park and decided to have some lunch. It will get warm soon, and I hope, by then, I will have found a place for her...

Richard stopped her. "Do you think they were thinking of us even then?" he asked.

"Probably not. We weren't even together." She thought of Paul and God then, and wondered at the stones she sometimes carried in her coat pocket. Listening, Trust, Optimism, Tenacity...She'd reached for the white stone only the other day, after her prayers. She hadn't seen God in quite some time, and she missed him, though she still felt his presence whenever she prayed and read His holy word. It was enough. She knew God was helping her.

April 22.

I'm done. Joy cries all the time. I can't keep her warm enough. I can't keep her fed enough. I can't keep her happy enough. I've left her at Safe Haven. It's been a week. Tom would never have allowed it. "You are a terrible mother, always passing the responsibility. You're no good."

I'd better stop crying or this page will be unreadable, as if that were really a problem. I don't know why I'm keeping this thing. Joy will never read it, I won't allow it. But I have to talk to someone.

Tom, how I miss him, but he is gone and it's my fault.

April.

I think it's still April. The buds are on the trees and I see a hint of new growth in the park where I am currently staying. There are friendly people here to offer a person whatever they need. Even what they don't. I won't speak of what I do to get what I want. I cannot speak of it.

May 10.

I need to see my daughter. When I went back for her yesterday, she cried. 'I missed you, Mommy!' And when I took her in my arms I knew I could never leave her again. The lady there, Jean Rasmussen, expects to see me and my daughter once a week. She says she expects that I'll allow my daughter a warm bath and a place to sleep.

Her words made me angry. The key is the only thing that kept me from screaming out at her. The key. How could such a simple thing keep a person going? But mother was always thinking of everyone, even me, even in death. She said, 'This key is yours,' in her last breath. 'Take it and remember who you are.' I'd already forgotten, but I knew my mother loved me, and that the treasure would be held in my heart forever...

"That's it for now," Virginia said. "So, what sort of jewelry box does the key fit?" She paused, and when Richard was silent she continued, "Why couldn't Grace have said 'the treasure is in the upstairs attic,' or something? Then we would have the box *and* Joy."

Richard laughed. "Oh, come on, Virginia. Even if she had, would we know any more than we know now? How many thousands of homes have attics?"

Virginia was embarrassed. Okay, so the clue would have to be more specific than that, so why didn't Grace give it? But maybe she had! "Remember who you are," she said out loud. Why do you think those words were so important?"

"She had a mother who wanted the best for her children."

"Right! But maybe there's a clue hidden in the words somewhere."

"You've got to be kidding." This time Richard rolled his eyes.

"I'm dead, I mean serious."

"Maybe the jewelry box is somewhere near a church. Perhaps, 'Remember who you are,' is something Grace heard every Sunday."

"Now you're really stretching," said Richard.

Virginia looked down at the worn, yellow cover. Then she looked again. With the front and back covers lying flat, the silver spiral circling down the center, she could see what had only appeared to be only random letters before. She wondered if Richard could see it.

**Property of: Grace Sorenson,
mother of Joy Sorenson,
in search of a better life this day,
February 1.**

and on the back:

R W Y A

Richard reached for the journal, and at the same time a small piece of paper, that had been shoved inside the spiral section of the notebook, fluttered to the floor.

Virginia picked it up. *Right Way Youth Academy,* it read.

Virginia showed the scrap to Richard.

"I guess you were wrong," he said, reaching for the piece and spreading it out on his leg. His eyes glowed. "Don't you think it's funny that *Remember Who You Are* and *Right Way Youth Academy* have the same first letters?"

***

Work at *Just Desserts* seemed to be calling for her, and they hadn't, as yet, discovered the meaning of the small note. Looking in the old phone directory had produced no results; neither had searching the name on the internet. But it had to be a place, or, at the very least, a clue to something.

The Gift – A Parable of the Key

March had rained some, and in its place new growth was springing forth in the city of Idaho Falls, Idaho, though it would be some time yet before the sun spent more than a few scattered moments warming her face.

Every time Virginia thought of Joy, she thought of Grace, and then her thoughts turned once again to the journal she and her husband had finished just last week. Sure enough, she and Richard had been spoken about in glowing terms, (and sometimes, not), but nothing else was said about the key or where the box had been buried. It was too bad they couldn't speak to Joy about the jewelry box. Perhaps she knew who the old man was, though maybe not. The girl had been wearing the key for awhile, and she had never seen the box amongst Joy's valuables - such as they were.

Virginia had begun to ask those who frequented *Just Desserts* if they'd heard of *Right Way Youth Academy*, and so far, had received only no's for answers.

And then it happened.

Virginia was serving God one April morning near Easter. That morning he said he needed at least a dozen pink cupcakes.

She'd smiled over at him, reached for the box, folded the corners up, and had begun to put the tasty treats inside when God added, "And you never know what one cupcake will mean over another."

"What?" Virginia gasped, stopping for a moment and peering at him through the glass. "What did you say?" She had meant it to come out kindly, though something else entirely had occurred.

73

"Cupcakes may even look the same on the outside, but often, it's the inside that gives us the real clue."

Now Virginia stood, six cupcakes filling the half empty box, and stared over at him. "If you have something to say, just say it," she said.

His blue eyes blinked. "Really, Virginia. All I need is another six cupcakes, and then I'll pay you for the order."

"But what did you mean about the insides?"

Richard peered at her from the back room. "Oh, hello," he said, walking into the room. Standing behind the counter he said, "I'd finish God's order if I were you."

God touched his fisherman's hat. "I have a lot of fishing to do today," he said. "And these cupcakes will come in handy."

Virginia gazed over at him and reached for the final six cupcakes. Placing them in the box, she creased the lid, shut it, and placed the box on the counter. "$20.50," she said.

"Your prices have gone up," God answered, handing Virginia the money.

"Sorry. New place. More bills."

God smiled, his eyes piercing her own. "Do you know what, Virginia? You get prettier by the day."

Virginia must have blushed. Richard stood near her and took her hand.

"Now I must go," said God. "See you soon?"
Virginia nodded.

***

"So, what do you think 'it's the inside that gives us the real clue' means?"

"God is a tricky one," Richard said.

They were standing in the lavender room. It was bare now of anything baby or child. A small couch sat in one corner and an end table held the yellow journal which had both wowed and confused them. And now this.

"Why do you think God wouldn't just tell me straight out where Joy is?"

"As I remember, you didn't even ask him," Richard said, taking her hand.

"That's right. All he could talk about was cupcakes. How one of them will be different from another one. He's so funny. He bought all pink cupcakes, with the same insides, and he...he just makes me crazy."

Richard laughed. "I think you're right about it being a clue. But you do know God. He wants you to search things out for yourself. Perhaps he figures it will mean more to you then, though I have no idea where he's going with this one."

"Remember that cake he brought to Trevor?"

"Sure. The stock boy ended up being Gail's boyfriend."

"Isn't it interesting that God always appears to use our shop to help someone else?"

"I never thought of that before," said Richard. "But maybe he doesn't - always. I mean, perhaps he uses our shop because that's what we do; that's how he teaches *us*."

Virginia looked out the large window where she'd long ago tossed the clothing and other baby items in anger. "Do you think," Virginia asked now, "that God is really saying that he has at least a dozen people that he's helping?"

"Well, at least that's what was going on today," said Richard. "But I can't help thinking there are more. You know, others that are shown the way back to him in different ways."

Virginia blinked. "What different ways?" she asked.

"Oh, I don't know. Oh, okay, suppose you're a doctor. How would God show a doctor what to do in life?"

"He might use a scalpel," Virginia prodded.

Richard frowned. "Seriously. How would God talk to a doctor?"

"Oh!" Suddenly Virginia was thinking of Paul. He was always getting sunflowers - sunflowers that grew taller than his house. And then a new thought entered her mind. "Sometimes they say it's a miracle when a certain patient lives. Have you ever wondered if there are times God directs the hands of a doctor?"

"Sure. Of course. But if you had to pick an object, what would it be?"

"I don't know, I guess I would just have to know the doctor. But I would probably use something meaningful, something that the doctor could see on a daily basis as a way of remembering Him. For us it's the stones, for Paul it was the sunflowers."

"Exactly!"

"So we are back to the start. What did God mean when he said, 'It's the inside that gives us the real clue?'"

"The inside. Perhaps we'll find *Right Way Youth Academy* within some other establishment."

***

Twenty-plus phone calls later, Virginia had a lead. Unfortunately, Richard was at *Just Desserts* and couldn't close up shop until 8:00. "So, why don't you check it out yourself," he said. "When I get home, we can discuss it together."

Virginia frowned on her side of the line but she knew that Richard was right. They had already closed up shop too many times the last few months to go in search of clues for Joy. It was time to settle down a little and make some profit.

And so she relented.

The church was just outside Idaho Falls. The journey was only a half hour drive south on I-15. Arriving in the city, Virginia stopped at Stockman's to get a bite to eat. The place was pleasing, though not fancy, and the waiter seemed too young to work there, though Virginia guessed he looked young because she was obviously getting older.

She smiled at herself and ordered a rib-eye. It was already 5:30, and the place would be closing in just half hour more, which seemed early to Virginia. After dinner, she'd venture to the Baptist church. Virginia hadn't stepped foot inside a church for years, but Pastor Rest seemed nice enough when she spoke with him on the phone.

A few minutes following her meal she was at the church. She spotted the cross on the small, white building, even before she discovered where to park. Soon enough she reached the doors and was knocking.

With a click of the handle the door opened, and a man wearing a regular white shirt and slacks asked, "Virginia?" His beard was filled with splotches of grey and his smile reminded Virginia of God's - warm and inviting.

"Yes. Thank you."

He instructed her to come inside.

The place was clean and orderly. She followed the pastor down one hall; then at the beginning of another. He led her inside a small room and asked her to sit down. The room looked like an office - probably his own. Pictures of Christ graced the walls, and a large wood cross hung on the wall behind the pastor's chair.

In moments he was asking her questions, and it wasn't easy to answer them, but she did. Answers about where she lived and what she did for a living were easy. The hard ones came after that. What church she attended and how God had helped her in her life. Virginia didn't want him to ask too many more of those, and when he didn't bring up the reason for her visit, she decided to speak up.

"Uh, Pastor. Could you tell me a little bit more about your program for teens?"

"Oh, yes." He stroked his beard. "That is the reason you came. But I need to tell you first off, it might have been better if you'd made an appointment with the pastor in Idaho Falls where you live - a shorter journey."

"I know, it's just...Well...I am in search of a missing girl."

Pastor Rest stroked his beard. "Who are you looking for?" he asked.

"A girl, 17 now, who may have attended *Right Way Youth Academy*. Joy...Joy Sorenson.

"Joy?" Now the man's face turned a striking white. "What do you need to know?" he asked. "Are you a family member?"

"No...a..."

"I can't give out any information unless you're a family member."

"I soon will be," Virginia said, trying to keep her voice calm though her heart was thundering in her chest. She hadn't considered this segment of the interview. "You see, we, my husband and I, have been trying to adopt Joy. Her mother died just a few months ago..."

"Her mother's, dead?" The pastor's voice echoed off the ceiling. "When?"

"In December."

"And the child is alone?"

"Somewhere. She was at *Safe Haven* for some time, and then one evening she went missing."

"I see. And Joy, how was she before she left the facility?"

"Fine, I guess. We wanted to bring her home but we were still in the paperwork process, the finalization of her foster care."

Pastor Rest was silent. He looked at her as if considering what his next words should be. Finally he said, "Well, Virginia, Miss Joy did take my class; a sort of camping experience where kids learn the art of the outdoors and the wonders of God. Unfortunately, after she graduated from the Academy, I didn't see her or her mother again. Of course, when the father left them..." The pastor frowned. "So, how can I help you now?" he asked, searching her eyes.

"A key was left with Joy upon the passing of her mother. My husband and I think the key is more than just a trinket handed down. Where the key is..."

"There will Joy be also," the pastor said, and Virginia instinctively thought of the scripture more than likely that had inspired the comment.

"I'm sure you know where they lived," Virginia said.

"Yes, but their home has since been demolished. Too many problems to fix, said the city. The place was, shall we say, brought down to nothing but wood and cement about two years ago."

"Oh." The news brought a shudder through Virginia. How would she find the girl now? And then the initials her mother had left on the outside of the journal as they related to the words inside came to her mind. "Do you know the meaning of 'remember who you are?'"

"Of course." The pastor laughed. "It was what we said during *Right Way Youth Academy* every morning the entire two weeks we were together. Why do you ask?"

"Well, we've learned some things about that slogan," Virginia began, trying to keep her voice calm and even. But the feat was difficult. When would she find Joy? Just talking to this pastor was taking precious time; and yet, she needed answers, and he appeared to be ready to send them her way.

Pastor Rest waited, and as Virginia gathered up renewed courage she said, "*Remember Who You Are*, is written in Grace's journal, an old yellow notebook we picked up from the center where they were occasionally staying. Inside the cover we found the place where we imagine the key was taped, and the words, '*Right Way Youth Academy*' on a small piece of paper within the spiral spine of the same journal. Important, don't you think?"

"I know they've been important to every teen and their parent going through the program," answered the pastor. "But I know for Joy and her mother, the words took on special significance. Seems Grace's own mother sort of passed the saying down from her mother."

"So what would the saying have to do with a key?"

"Grace was a collector of sorts, if I'm remembering correctly," he wiped his beard, "she was the one who always initiated the craft days here, though she wasn't one to take on the cooking. So how were Joy and her mother getting along the last time you saw them?"

"Homeless. Grace was into drinking and drugs. I don't know about Joy."

"Probably the same. But you never know, she and her mother made some pretty firm commitments while in the Academy - commitments they weren't suppose to take on lightly, though I know how the world is."

"So they attended together?"

"It was a mother and daughter event in the summer. During early fall we did the same thing with fathers and sons. The program is still going famously, though I have stepped back a little since then." He rubbed his beard.

***

"So the pastor knew her?"

"Yes. And he knew about the program and he knew about the saying between Joy and her mother. And of course he knew their address."

"Did you drive by?"

"Yes, but it was too dark and I couldn't see anything but rubble. Let's go tomorrow. *Just Desserts* will be closed and we can spend some time together in daylight searching the area.

***

Virginia had been right. The place was only rubble. One couldn't even tell if a house had been there before. And yet, there were still homes across the street - old, decrepit dwellings that Virginia could only imagine also housed rodents and bed bugs, which did little to assuage her fears.

Still, perhaps in the rubble they would find the jewelry box. Highly un-likely, but one had to check out these things. Joy wasn't in sight, and thoughts of her all alone somewhere, or maybe hooked up with some 'loser' drifted in and out of Virginia's mind like a dark cloud. Even if they found the box, they didn't have the key to open it; and they didn't have Joy.

The Gift – A Parable of the Key

The place where the house once stood was a mess. Plenty of 'someones' had already scrounged the area for trinkets, and mostly what was left was old rusted house parts, twisted metal and broken down fencing. A shiny piece of paper caught her eye. Only a gum wrapper. Another piece a bit larger. Someone's castaway homework.

"Find anything?" she yelled to her husband, who was looking through something near the front sidewalk.

"Just junk," he yelled back. "Maybe the neighbors know something." He looked across the street, just as she had done when they'd first entered the neighborhood, only to see someone in a long overcoat approach them.

"So what 'cha be a 'wanting?" the old man asked, shuffling to a stop. He wore old loafers and a battered hat. Virginia had already joined her husband when she'd seen the man coming.

"Know the woman who lived here?" he asked, pointing to the rugged spot.

"Everyone knew Grace," he said. "Everyone." He planted his worn hands in his threadbare pant pockets. "So what 'cha be a wanting?" he asked again.

"Information," chimed in Virginia. The man visibly jumped. He must not have seen her.

"You together?" he asked.

Virginia nodded. "What would a couple of young folks want to know about a woman and her daughter? You know he left them."

"The husband."

"Yep. Never liked the fool. Never took enough care of his wife and child. I told him so on more than one occasion. You a relative or something?"

"Hope to be, for Joy," Richard said before she could stop him. It probably wasn't wise to share everything, especially those things that might not come to fruition anyway, and especially if they never found her.

"Then you must be related to the mother." He scuffed his old shoe against the cement and looked deeply into her eyes as if trying to figure out what she was trying not to tell him.

"We're not related," said Virginia.

"But you said..."

Virginia nudged Richard but he must not have gotten the hint. "We'll be adopting Joy. The mother was found dead this winter."

"Dead?" The old man's mouth suddenly crumbled. A small tear escaped his right eye. "When they left, I thought for sure they'd come back and visit but they never did. The place was finally torn down. I haven't seen the husband in years - good riddance; but the wife and child, well, I took right kindly to both of them. The girl must be, what now?"

"Seventeen."

The man whistled and removed his hands from his trousers. Rubbing them together he said, "You know, it's right cold out here. Want to come in for some tea?"

Virginia smiled.

***

The Gift – A Parable of the Key

The old man opened the heavy apricot colored curtains hanging in the kitchen and began to prepare some tea. "My wife, Dove, was with me for some years and she was right fond of that little girl. When Joy would visit they would have milk and cookies in the dining room (he pointed to a small room with a table just opposite the kitchen) and talk about life. "But I have forgotten myself, my name is John."

"Nice to meet you, John," Richard said, extending his hand, which John shook vigorously. Virginia reached forth her own hand, but this time John took it gently, lifted it to his wrinkly lips, and kissed it.

Virginia must have blushed because Richard was giggling.

"Now I've forgotten myself once again," John continued, releasing her hand and returning to the stove. "A man in my days was always quite respectful when a lady was in the room."

"So what did you think about Grace?" Virginia asked.

"Oh, she was high class, even with that retch of a husband. Had a drinking problem, that one, and when things got even more impossible, my wife told Grace to leave him. But she wouldn't. She was of the religious persuasion and said she was going to work things out. Of course that never happened. The man left her before much could be worked out."

The old man brought the tea kettle over. The tea bags already sat in a small bowl in front of her. He returned to the stove and reached for the cups hanging on little hooks above him. "He more than likely left because of his drinking."

Virginia looked at her husband. She poured the hot liquid in her cup and reached for a bag. Placing it in the heated water, she watched as John sat down beside her husband at the table. "I'm glad you folks stopped by," the man said, pouring the hot water into his own cup and reaching for a tea bag.

It was funny, though it shouldn't have been. The man was kind, though they hadn't come to visit him at all.

Richard filled his cup and placed another tea bag. "So, is that why Grace left the house? Because her husband left her?"

"Mostly," the man answered, swirling the tea bag with his spoon. "She couldn't afford the place. Said she'd gotten a small apartment for her and the child. So where are they now?"

Virginia took out her tea bag and placed it on a small plate that was already on the table. "Like we told you, the mother is dead."

"Grace is dead?" John's mouth crumbled once more and another tear escaped his eye. "And the little girl, how old is she now?"

"Seventeen."

"Seventeen. And where is she living?" He removed the bag, added it to Virginia's plate, and took a sip. "I love this herbal stuff," he said. "We couldn't feed it to Joy, just milk. But she sure loved cookies."

Richard took his own sip and looked intently at Virginia. What he couldn't say in words, Virginia already knew.

"We are hoping to adopt Joy," she said now, placing her cup back on the table and smiling over at the old man. "But she has run away."

"What have you done?" the man hollered, dropping his cup. The liquid splattered on the table in front of them.

"Please, please," Richard said. "We didn't do anything. The girl ran away from the shelter."

"What shelter?" the man asked, slowly maneuvering his body to the kitchen sink and grabbing a paper towel. "I have to watch things, really watch things." He returned, towel in hand and bent to mop the spill.

"Let me help," Richard said, but the man was already waving him away. "Since my dear Dove's death, I have had to do many *womanly* things." He smiled. "So what about this shelter. Are you telling me that Grace and her daughter were homeless?"

He walked back to the stove and opened a cabinet where he deposited the paper towel. "Now," he continued, returning to the same spot at the table and refilling his cup, "tell me what is happening to Grace and her daughter."

Virginia took a deep breath and started from the beginning, relaying to the old man all their concerns about where Joy was, now that she had run away, where they had looked so far, and who might know where she was today. But John was quiet.

"If I'd only known," he said. "Dove and I...we...when she was here..." Another tear glistened in his eye. "We would have taken them in. But Grace, she was a proud woman, a very proud woman."

"A key was left for Joy by her mother. Do you know anything about that?" It was a sudden move, but John was likely to forget again and they'd have to clue him in, beginning all over again.

"A key? Why, yes, I remember a key. Grace wore it around her neck; would let no one touch it, not even that horrible husband of hers. I asked her about it once and she said it was...it was...oh yes, the *key to her heart*. I asked her what it fit. She said, 'Oh, you don't want to know about that.' But I did want to know and so did Dove. We both wanted to know."

"So what did the key fit?"

"She had a saying about the key. She was to remember something."

"Remember who you are?" Virginia prodded.

"That's it!" hollered the man, placing his cup down and standing. "I have something to show you," he said.

Ten minutes later the man hadn't returned. "Do you think we should go after him?" Virginia asked.

"Either that or have the man forget why he went down the hall in the first place," Richard answered.

They stood and together traveled down the long hall, past one pink bathroom and what appeared to be a guest room on the left. Near the end of the hall they found John, sitting on his bed, an antique bronze jewelry box sitting on his lap. He looked up. "Oh, it's you," he said.

Virginia sighed with relief.

The Gift – A Parable of the Key

The man caressed the old box. It was exquisite. The lid and sides appeared to be decorated with interesting scenes of life.

"It's French Nouveau," said the man. "Quite expensive. For years I wondered why Grace left the box to me and my wife, but now, now I wonder if it had something to do with her daughter. You have the key, I hope."

"Joy has the key."

The man touched the engravings on the box, slowly, as if trying to remember something. "We can't damage it. It must have the key."

"Are you sure you haven't seen Joy? She hasn't come by for a visit?" Even as she said the words Virginia knew it was highly possible that Joy *had* come by but the man might not be able to remember.

"Joy hasn't visited me in years," John said, laying the box on the back side and looking at the key hole. "I always wondered why I'd get such a box if Grace was always going to have the key, but she told me to keep it safe, that she couldn't bring it with her. Had a fear of it getting lost or stolen."

John lifted it slowly and returned it to its place by the side of the bed. "I'm sorry."

The words sounded so final, and Virginia couldn't stand it. "Do you have any idea where Joy may have gone?"

"I wish she'd come here," he said, standing, and directing them to the door. "I wish she'd come here."

Back in the kitchen, Virginia helped John clear the cups and place them in the sink. "I'll wash them out later," he said.

Virginia and her husband turned to leave. No, they didn't have Joy, but they knew where the jewelry box was and that was something. "Did Joy know her mother gave you the jewelry box?" she asked.

"I'm not sure," the man answered. "Do you really have to leave? I can get you something else."

"Thank you for the tea," Virginia offered, "but we really need to know if Joy knew her mother left the jewelry box with you."

"I said I'm not sure." Suddenly, the man looked angry. "Why would you want to know about that old box?" he asked just as quickly. "Who are you, and how did you get inside my house?"

Richard reached for the old doorknob and opened the door. Taking Virginia's hand he ushered her out.

Virginia didn't know what to think, and Richard, well, he was beyond words.

***

"Some kind of memory loss, I guess," said Virginia.

"Definitely. The man shouldn't be living alone. I wonder where his family is?"

As they traveled home Virginia couldn't help but think of the two puzzle pieces that had finally led them to the French box. It was a beautiful thing, not easy to get one's hands on, especially in Idaho, and yet, hadn't the box come from Grace's mother?

"Grace's mother must have had some money," Virginia said now, watching the whiteness of covered trees as they sped past.

"I thought the same thing. It's too bad we don't know where Grace's mother lived."

"Why?"

"Perhaps we could track down Joy that way. Her mother is dead, but perhaps the current occupants of her childhood home would know about her."

"If her place isn't torn down as well."

Richard's eyes turned to her briefly and then back to the road. "I don't think so. If the box is any indication of the interests of Grace's mother, it may be safe to say she lived in some classical rendition."

Virginia laughed. "Rendition?"

"Why sure." Virginia watched the ends of Richard's mouth curl up into a smile. "And consider this. If not Grace's mother, then her mother. The woman may have even come from France."

"Like that's going to help."

"It might. Every little clue helps, Virginia. In time we'll have enough to find Joy and bring her home."

Virginia imagined, just for a moment, traipsing around France. Well, that was highly unlikely. They might find the long lost house, but Joy would have never been able to afford the trip.

***

It was May when a phone message arrived from *Safe Haven*. It was short and sweet. "We've found Joy," said Jean. Virginia had been so busy at work, she hadn't checked the phone until now. She was teaching another marriage class and it had just ended, the final stragglers leaving and giving her a moment's breath. It was 2:15 and the message had been left around noon.

"We've got to go, now!" she screamed to Richard. He was in the back room, and something tumbled to the ground.

"What fell?"

"Just a canister. What's up?" He was wiping his hands against a *Just Desserts* apron as he entered the room.

"Joy. They've found her!"

If she lived to be a hundred years old, she would remember the day she and her husband closed down the store early and raced to *Safe Haven*. Stop lights that hadn't been there before appeared out of nowhere, and once, only once mind you, they'd been followed by a police officer. Virginia had forced herself to slow down. "We'll never get there!" she finally screeched, only to have her husband reply: "We won't if you aren't careful."

Her brow furrowed, they continued to *Safe Haven*, and once there, raced into the building. Her anxious face must have looked like a giant red apple, but she didn't care. Breathing in and out like an accordion on steroids she raced to the front desk.

Jean smiled over at her. "Finally," she said, "the girl has been driving me crazy!"

In their attempt to get inside quickly they'd completely missed Joy, standing by the door.

Seeing Joy for the first time she raced over. But Richard was quicker. In no more time than it would take a lap dog to reach its owner, Richard had scooped her up in his arms and was spinning her around. "Oh, Joy!" he screamed again and again. He was laughing and crying. Virginia was laughing and crying. Joy was silent.

"Stop," she said. "Put me down. I'm not...two."

It was like an electric bolt had entered Richard's heart. "Sorry," he said, pulling her back away from him.

Joy brushed at her torn sweatshirt, muddied and worn. She looked up at them. "Yes, as you can see, I'm back." She tried to smile. "I've never seen you so excited."

Virginia looked down at Joy's pants and shoes and the mud that had accumulated underneath her fingernails.

"I've been waiting here too long," she said. "I almost went to get a shower, but I didn't want to miss you," she said.

"See what I mean?" said Jean, approaching them. "This...girl seems to think that a shower could wait. I'm not so sure."

"So you waited all this time to see us?"

"Sure. What else was I supposed to do? You're my parents, right?"

Virginia could hardly think. Her heart was melting into a thousand pieces and she wasn't sure how she would ever be able to gather them up again.

Joy

"Why did you leave?" The question was abrupt, Virginia knew it, but it had to be asked. As the girl squirmed in her chair at *Safe Haven*, Virginia tried to be patient. Richard sat beside her and Joy across from them, lightly touching each of their hands at different times as she spoke.

"I missed my mother," she said. "I missed her so much!"

Joy's hands reached up to her eyes and she sobbed, rivulets of dirt and grime making their way down her cheeks. "I went to see her, the place where she was buried. I even stole some flowers from someone's yard, they were practically dead, but I..." She sobbed some more, and then wiping at her eyes, looked into the faces of Virginia and Richard.

"I had to do it," she said. "I had to find out." Another short sob escaped her throat before she continued. "You wouldn't understand."

Virginia wondered if she would. The child, a teen now, was obviously upset that her mother was gone, and she'd gone out in search of...something. Some healing, perhaps. A way back.

Richard reached for the girl. "We probably wouldn't understand," he said, "so why don't you tell us."

Joy blinked, the last of the muddy tears drying on her cheeks. "You promise not to get angry?"

Virginia swallowed. Richard was silent. "We promise," he said.

"I was only going to find the grave at first, but things got cold, so I made my way over to *Just Desserts.* It was Sunday, and I knew you wouldn't be there. Sorry," she added lamely.

Virginia couldn't help but think about how accurate they'd been in looking for her. It was almost as if someone had spoken in their ears, and she'd known what to do, albeit a little too late.

"When I couldn't get in I got angry. I almost came back here, but I couldn't. The waiting for you was just too hard! I thought...I could get a good job, or something, and that it would be easier for you to take me in, especially when I turned eighteen and should really be on my own." She paused, took a breath, and continued: "I know you would have taken care of me, but I'm not a baby, and...and I wanted to be sure I was doing the right thing in having you adopt me."

So that was it.

"I didn't want you to take me in just because my mom wanted it. I wanted to do it because it was the right thing. My mother always said, 'Remember who you are,' and I was trying to remember who I really was!"

Virginia covered her mouth, quickly. She felt a sob coming on and wanted the girl to continue. Richard was still silent.

Joy reached for the necklace. She pulled it from underneath her sweatshirt and looked down at the key on the strand. "This was my mother's," she said, "but it was also my grandmother's. My grandmother kept a beautiful box of secret things; I've never been told what she kept, and when she was close...to death, she gave the box to my mother. I don't know what she was supposed to do with it, but I wondered if she'd put some secret things in it, too. And now it's mine," she said, placing the necklace back behind the old sweatshirt. "Only I have no idea where the box is. I've read her journal over and over and all I know is that it was given to some old geezer. Why would my mother do that?"

"Maybe she had a reason," Virginia offered.

"I wish I had it," the girl breathed. "I mean, there's got to be some treasure inside, right?"

Virginia swallowed.

But Joy was standing. "I think it's about time I had a shower," she said, picking at her soiled shirt. "I probably stink, too. Can you wait for me?"

"Sure. Get your shower. We have something to share with you as well," Richard said, touching Virginia lightly on the arm.

***

Joy wore a clean blue shirt and new jeans and on her feet, toe socks. Each toe was a different color, and as she wiggled them, sitting on the same chair she'd left just twenty minutes prior, Virginia and Richard couldn't help but laugh. So this was part of tenacity...Responding to the fun as well as the turmoil and pain. Virginia's eyes canvassed the girl's green eyes. Her blond hair was wet, and lying at her shoulders in thick rivulets. For the first time she noticed that the slight girl was becoming a woman, too. How could she have missed it?

"So, what were you going to tell me?" she asked, placing her hands in front of her and looking eagerly at them both.

"We have some good news," said Richard, reaching for her. "We know where the jewelry box is."

In all of her life, Virginia could not have prepared herself for the response that came next. It was almost like a piece of sunlight had shot between them, as if in hearing the words, 'jewelry box', Joy, was finally able to reveal her true self.

"I don't believe it!" she sang, standing up and hugging them both. They still sat in their chairs. "You really have the box? Where did you find it? Is it still in one piece? Is it dirty, or ruined or anything?"

She sat, her breath coming out quickly, her legs trembling like a reed.

"We don't have it, exactly," said Virginia, remembering the cold departure from John. "But I think we can get it." Even as she said the words, Virginia hoped that she was right. She hoped in the deepest part of her soul that she and Richard's previous visit to see John would be remembered.

***

"And what would you be a' wanting?" John asked. Amazingly, the man wore the same clothes, though his partially bald head of hair seemed combed. He peered over at Joy. "And who are you?" he asked.

"Joy, you remember me, Mr. ah Franklin."

The man didn't smile. He glared.

On the drive over they had discussed John as the old man in the journal, though Joy had surprisingly admitted that she'd never thought of him as the *old man*. She'd told them how strange it had been to be in his house, how warm and unreal it had always been - like going to heaven without really going there. "Perhaps that's why I never thought of him as the *old man*. He was more like God," she'd told them.

And now they were here. And the man wasn't sounding anything like God.

He opened the screen. "What are you selling?" he hollered.

"Surely you remember us," Richard prodded. Virginia squirmed.

"What are you selling?" the man asked again. "I don't need a vacuum and I don't need any of that orange cleaner. Besides, you were here last week trying to sell me that stuff. So how much is it? I might just pay you for it so's you'll get out of my hair."

Virginia thought again of the man's hair and his messy wardrobe, and then tried to focus on his eyes. They weren't getting anywhere.

"You remember, John, you showed us the jewelry box the last time we were here," Virginia said.

The Gift – A Parable of the Key

"And look!" said Joy, releasing the key from underneath her shirt. "Here is the key!"

The man blinked and then he sputtered. "Where did you get that?!" he yelled. "Grace wouldn't have let that out of her sight. Where is Grace?" He looked around the screen door as if expecting to see her. The man's lips trembled, and as they stood on the porch, waiting for John's reply, she knew that his words could go either way. Either he would finally see or they would be brushed off the porch like the last time.

"Grace, my mother, is gone, Mr. Franklin."

"Gone, gone where?" was the answer.

Joy reached for the screen door, and, holding it with her left hand, reached out with her right to John. "She's dead. I'm Joy, her daughter."

If she lived to be a hundred years old, Virginia would never forget what happened next. The old man looked into Joy's eyes and it was as if a cloud had moved from his eyes. He smiled. "Joy? But you have grown, child!"

He took her hand, and looking into her eyes, kissed her sweetly on the cheek. "I have waited for you," he said.

A small tear found its way down Joy's cheek. "And I have been looking for you," she said. "Can we come in?"

"Why, sure, sure!" John sang, opening the inner door for all of them. "Richard! Virginia! When did you get here?" he asked.

They stood in the living room and all was the same, the same as they'd left it just a few weeks previous; except for two things. Joy was with them and she had the key.

***

In John's room, Virginia's and Richard's eyes turned to the place where the box had sat, but it was no longer there. "I almost forgot," said the man, turning to face them, his lips turned down at the corners. "Tom, he was here. He demanded to see the box." The man's voice shook. "I'm s...sorry."

"What man?" Virginia asked. "Who is Tom?"

John looked squarely into Joy's eyes and the girl was silent. Still, there appeared to be some recognition in her large green eyes. "He was here?" she asked.

"I had to give it to him," John said, sitting on the bed, and patting a place next to him. But Joy didn't move. "I told him he couldn't have it, that it wasn't his. I should have never let him in. He was going to tell me where Grace was, and you." He looked up at the girl who was standing like solid rock before him. "He...promised."

"He lied," Joy sobbed.

The man patted the spot next to him. This time Joy relented. She sat with her head bowed, tears streaming down her cheeks.

"Who is Tom?" Virginia asked again.

"Yes, who is he?" Richard offered.

The room was as still as night, without a cloud, without a star.

"Joy's father," said John. "He was here."

100

Joy looked up. The happiness that had once shined from hers eyes was gone. Tears wetted her cheeks. "Everyone hated my dad, including me."

"His parents?"

"No, they didn't hate him. Thought he was perfect, I'm sure. Dead now."

"Other family?"

"I don't know. If he had them he never spoke about them."

Virginia was silent. What could she possibly say? How could this girl go on knowing her father held the secret to her mother's heart?

***

"We'll find it, that's all there is to it," said Virginia, her arm wrapped lovingly around the girl's shoulders. They sat in the back of the car as Richard drove. As the girl cried, Virginia's thoughts whirled. They had spoken with most of the neighbors after leaving John. Nothing. This time John remembered them all the way to the door, but he was sad, and Virginia knew, lonely.

"My father kept pretty much to himself," Joy said now, looking down at the blue and white tennis shoes covering her colorful toe socks. "When he left, no one cared."

The roads cleared as the day wore on to afternoon, and by evening, as the air grew chill, Richard, Virginia and Joy returned to *Safe Haven*, only to have to leave her again.

The Box

The following few weeks blew by like spring, and neither she nor Richard had learned anything about Joy's father, Tom. "Maybe we should forget about the whole thing," Richard said one evening after they'd returned Joy to the shelter. "Maybe..."

"Maybe, nothing," said Virginia, looking at the stones still gracing the mantel of their living room. "What do you think constancy means anyway? God has shown us the way, all this time. Do you think he's going to stop helping us now?"

Richard moaned. "Really, Virginia. Maybe we're not supposed to get that old box. Maybe having Joy with us is enough. The paperwork is almost finished as well as the visits here. And the classes..."

"Without that box, it will never be enough for Joy, can't you see that?"

Richard placed the Bible on the end table. Just the week previous they had decided to attend church. The experience had been refreshing, but without Joy, who said she felt 'funny' about church, things were strained and more than a bit difficult. Still, there would have been lots of questions from those attending services, so perhaps it was just as well.

"I don't know where we're going to look," said Richard. "We have less to go on with him than we ever had to go on when it came to Joy."

"What about that preacher? The one we met just outside Idaho Falls?"

"You mean, you met," Richard corrected.

Virginia thought back. "Right. He said something about Joy's father in the mix. Right as I was leaving the pastor said something that really didn't matter much to me then. But now... He said Joy's father had driven them to and from the Academy. They hadn't come themselves. Why he said he remembered the incident was because Tom was huffing and puffing about having to drive them over on a Thursday night - his night."

"That's interesting. Perhaps it was his drinking night..."

"And maybe they only had one car," Virginia offered. "Or maybe Gracc didn't have a driver's license. She didn't have one with her when she died."

"You're right. Perhaps we can learn more from this preacher, uh...Pastor Rest. Up for a visit?"

Half an hour later they'd reached the small church, but Virginia hadn't called ahead. It was Monday and the place appeared empty. They'd decided to close up shop at *Just Desserts*, and hoped the already slow business they usually received on Mondays would be the standard fare today; in other words, not too many disappointed customers.

"Now what?" Virginia asked her husband, who was a few feet away from her and checking doors. "I don't think you should be doing that. Besides," she looked around the parking lot, "no cars."

"Maybe he lives close and can walk." He walked around the church. A few minutes later Richard hadn't returned, so she went after him. The door at the back was unlocked. She entered and made her way around the long hall until she heard voices. Yes, her husband was inside and so was someone else.

"Been talking to your husband," said an old gent, twice the age of the pastor. He wore gray overalls and a fisherman's cap. "God?" she stumbled.

"Well, hello, Virginia. How have you been?"

"You're cleaning a church?" she couldn't help asking. A broom was against one wall, and it looked like God was gathering up the large bucket for mopping. "Why, sure. Looking for Pastor Rest?" he asked.

Virginia was dumbfounded. Okay, sure, she'd seen God in her kitchen and at the grocery store and at *Just Desserts* but at a church? And then she couldn't help laughing at herself. Of course God was at a church; where else would God be?

"Sorry, Virginia. I got so busy talking that I forgot to tell you I'd found my way in." Richard looked at her and offered his arm. She took it. It was much easier to stand with support. "I've been talking to God about Joy and her father, and he's given me..."

"Why didn't you tell me that Joy's father was still alive?" Virginia interrupted. She shouldn't have interrupted, but there it was.

"You didn't ask me," God answered. "Besides, haven't you had some fun learning on your own, with just a nudge here and there?"

"I would hardly call it...fun," Virginia said, her voice croaking a bit. "But we did meet John."

"Oh yes, John," God said, reaching within the closet and turning on the low faucet inside to fill the bucket. The water splashed and whirled, and the bucket, once filled, was rolled out the door. "John is one of my best servants." He smiled.

Virginia's breath left her for a moment as she looked at God and God looked at her. God loved her, she knew that without question, but did she love God as he loved her?

"I'm interested to know how you've been faring with the five stones," asked God, placing the mop in the bucket and leaning the handle against the wall.

She almost began, "Well, you know..." but checked herself. The reason she talked with God wasn't because he didn't know what was going on in her life; she prayed to him so that she might connect with him. "I've been using the five stones, religiously," she said, grinning a bit because of the pun that had managed to break forth from her lips.

"I'm glad to hear that," God answered, "but your listening could improve some. Remember, I always like to hear questions. Trust me, I know all of the answers."

Now God was getting into the act.

"I'm optimistic about that," said Virginia, trying not to laugh, but it was true. She was optimistic about all God had to offer her. She was glad that she hadn't given up on him or on Joy or her husband. The tenacity had paid off in all accounts and she was glad that her life was a constant (or practically constant) life with God. "So what have you been telling Richard?"

God reached for the bucket. "I've got a lot of mopping to do," he said. "Maybe your husband can relay the message."

For the first time since she'd entered the room, Virginia really looked at it. The room was large, and was probably used for family events. There was no carpet to speak of, just a shiny yellow floor with scuff marks in places that God would obviously be cleaning up.

Virginia smiled over at God, thanked him, and turned to Richard. "So, what did God tell you?" she asked. She watched from the corner of her eye as God squeezed the mop-head into the bucket and went about cleaning the first section of the dirty floor.

"I've been praying for days that we'd get an answer," Richard said. "But I never expected to find God here."

"I've been praying, too, but nothing came."

"I don't know what did it, but it might have been the question I asked."

"What question?"

"Well, I was reading in the Bible that passage, 'Behold, I stand at the door and knock...'"

"I know that one."

"Well, I was reading and suddenly it came to me like a burst of light. God wants to talk with us - even have a conversation, but first we must be willing to open the door! He reminded me of the experience today."

"And?"

"Don't you get it?"

Virginia didn't have a clue.

"Joy's father was here, at this very church with the old jewelry box, looking for the key that Joy has!"

"God told you that?"

"Not exactly. He said Joy's father had visited with the pastor just two days ago, and I thought to myself, what sort of questions would Tom ask?'

The answer was easy. "About the key, of course. But why would Joy's father need the key? He could have just destroyed the box to get what's inside."

"I wondered the same thing. God said to trust him."

Trust? Virginia felt suddenly frustrated. "So where is Joy's father?"

Richard frowned. "I think he was just about to tell me when you walked in."

Virginia could feel the warmth rise in her cheeks. She looked over toward the corner where God had begun his mopping, but he was gone. She surveyed the floor. It was clean.

***

"So, what was the question you asked God?"

In the kitchen, Richard was fixing dinner. She loved it when he fixed dinner. It always reminded her of how handy men could be in the kitchen when they wanted to be.

"Oh, I asked him how I could best help you, and he told me that I needed to always be open to your suggestions."

"Why that question?" Virginia asked. Richard stirred the chili - his own recipe - that was never the same each time he cooked it.

"I don't know. I guess I was thinking about what kind of conversation I would like to have with God and I thought of the conversations I have with you. I wanted it to be like that."

A sweet warmth traveled up her back and arms but she didn't speak.

"You know, Virginia, the relationship we have with God can be a lot like the one *we* have. I don't know why it has taken me so long to figure it out, but I'm glad I'm finally getting it. We don't have to climb a tower to reach God, we don't even have to go up into the mountains. All we need to do is ask, wherever we are."

Virginia watched as he brought the bowls and cups to the table and then the large hot pad where the chili rested, still in the pot. A large green spoon poked out from the top. Richard had also brought to the table grated cheese and a pitcher of water. "Would you like to say the prayer?" he asked.

Virginia bowed her head. "Dear God," Virginia prayed. "Can you help us know thy will concerning Joy? Help us to know where to look for the box. Help us to love each other. Bless Joy. And bless this food. Amen."

***

Joy giggled. "I've figured it out," she said. "Yesterday, after you left I sat down and wrote a list of all of the places my father went. I thought of all the places he took me, and then a new thought came to me. I was eating dinner when all of a sudden the answer came."

Virginia's skin prickled.

"The first Thursday of the month when I was little my father wouldn't come home until very late. It was his 'bar' night, he said, and so mother and I watched one of my favorite shows on television or rented a movie. Dad wasn't home when I went to bed but I remember hearing him about 2 a.m., as he slipped through the front door.

"One night, when I was a little older, I worked it out with mom to follow him. She didn't like the idea, but I'd been pestering her for weeks. 'I don't want you near a bar,' she said, and I'd promised we would only sit in the car and watch him go in. I think in the back of my mind I knew there was something else going on besides the bar and so did my mother, and so one Thursday she relented and we followed him. But dad didn't go to the bar, at least not that night. We followed him all the way to the city cemetery, can you believe it?"

Virginia swallowed. "So why the cemetery?" she asked.

"My grandfather and grandmother, the ones who gave my mother the antique jewelry box and key, are buried there."

"But aren't they your mother's mother and father?"

"Yes, and we thought that was a bit strange, and so we watched him. He walked to their graves and placed flowers on each one and stood there for just a little while before heading back to the car. After that he went to the bar. We went home after that but the following month we followed him out again. He did the same thing."

"Perhaps he missed your mother's parents."

"That's the strange part," said Joy, brushing her thin fingers through her wet hair. "He hated them. Don't you think it's funny that he'd want to visit their graves?"

"Funny doesn't begin to cover it," said Richard. "Unless there was something at the gravesite that Tom wanted to get an answer to."

"Like what?"

"Yeah, like what?" Virginia echoed.

"Before your father left you and your mother, what kind of interest did he have in the jewelry box?"

"I don't know," Joy shrugged. "I mean, it sat in my parent's bedroom on the dresser; but as far as I knew, mom always wore the key around her neck so he couldn't have even peeked inside. Do you think he heard about mother's death?"

"Well, that would be the only reason to search for the box now," said Richard. "And the key." He stood, waving them to sit in their chairs while he spoke with Jean.

She was all smiles today. "The paperwork is about ready," she said now as he approached.

"Good," said Richard, almost shrugging off her comment for what he was about to ask her. "Jean, has an older gentleman been around here lately asking about Joy?"

"An older man, no, I don't think so."

He turned to Joy and waved her over. "What does the man look like?" he asked.

"The man?" Joy hesitated for only a moment. "Dark hair the last time I saw him. He wasn't fat or anything, just big, you know. Brown eyes."

Jean frowned. "Sorry," she said. "Who is it you're looking for?"

"My...a this man who has been following me around."

"That's pretty scary," said Jean.

Virginia could hear the conversation from where she was sitting and was glad Joy had received the hint about keeping her father's name a secret. Still, Jean and those working at *Safe Haven* would have to know that the father was alive at some point, and Virginia just didn't want to think about that.

***

The cemetery they entered at dusk was not as well kept up as the one that Joy's mother had been buried in; still, it was good to know that Joy remembered the spot where her grandparents had been buried, having visited a few times with her mother.

The graves were nestled under a wide-spread tree on top of a fairly large hill. Unfortunately, however, there was nothing to block the quick winds or the darkness that would soon be enveloping them.

Fortunately there was a bench close by where they sat.

Permission had been granted from *Safe Haven* for a one-night sleep over, though Virginia wondered now if keeping the girl up all hours of the night had been the best choice. But Joy seemed happy enough. They'd brought along hot chocolate and doughnuts, and there was always the car if things got too cold outside.

They talked about Joy's early days with her parents, when life was happy - before the drinking had begun with both of her parents and before her father had left them. It was easy to see that Joy had loved her father once, loved their vacations together, the sweet way he lifted her up into his arms to piggy back her around the yard, their meals together.

And then, something had happened. Her mother had found someone else. Joy thought her father had gotten ill, but now that she was older and could think back on it, Joy knew that her father had become an alcoholic. If it hadn't been for her mother taking to the habit after him, and not handling the liquor as he had, he might even today be with her; but her mother's uncontrollable drinking had been the last straw.

"I can't believe he left mother for the same thing he was doing," Joy said now, "but he did, and maybe it's the best thing he could have ever done. I was drinking then, too."

"And drugs?" Virginia asked now as the night grew even more chill.

"Drugs? I never tried the needle," said Joy. "My mother was too protective. Even at your house..." Her voice droned on, and she looked away from the flashlight that Richard had just snapped on. "I'm so sorry. I told mother that she should have thrown them out before coming to your place, but she liked it too much by that time."

"As long as you didn't try them, that's all that matters," said Richard, flicking off the light suddenly and staring out into the distance where they'd parked the car. "I think someone's coming," he said, though Virginia hadn't heard anything.

They stood in unison, and taking their cups of chocolate with them, walked behind the large tree. It couldn't shelter them, at least not completely, but it was dark after all. And then Virginia noticed a faint light flashing, bouncing, until finally it stopped.

Joy gasped. "It's got to be him," she whispered. "What do we do now?"

Richard was silent. So was Virginia. They watched, as what appeared to be a man, knelt down and began whispering to the grave. They were too far away to hear it, but he was definitely speaking. Virginia's arms suddenly chilled and she wondered how much longer they would be able to stay out in this late, wintery night, if it wasn't him.

"What if it's not him?" Virginia asked, wrapping her coat tightly around her body.

"It's got to be him. Who else would want to visit my grandparents' grave this late at night? I'll go." Joy left them suddenly and began her walk to the graves just a few feet away. Virginia and Richard followed closely behind.

The large form was still pressing his hands on the grave where Joy's grandparents were buried, when

Joy approached. Something was placed on the stone. A shudder like the beginnings of a storm creased the air.

"I'm so sorry," said the man to no one. "I have lost it. I have lost *her*."

"Father?" Joy's voice was small in the large space, and the air grew suddenly quiet.

"Who's there?" The man stumbled to his feet. Virginia wondered if he was drunk or if the surprise had momentarily startled him.

"Father. I'm here."

The man turned his flashlight to the girl's face. She winced.

"Joy?" he offered. "What are you doing here?"

"Same as you. Visiting."

"It's near 1 a.m. Where are you staying?"

"The shelter."

"I knew it. So your mother is truly gone."

"Yes."

"And you are alone."

"Not completely, Father."

"The shelter. You shouldn't be staying there."

"I know, but it won't be for long. I will be eighteen soon."

The flashlight's beam traveled the length of the girl's body and rested at her feet. "I can't believe it. Pastor Rest said..."

"Father, why are you in search of mother's box?" The question was abrupt, and Virginia's heart pounded waiting for Tom's response.

"What box?"

"The jewelry box you swiped. Where is it?"

"It's not the old man's."

"Where is it?"

"Safe. Why do you care?"

"It was left to me."

"I thought I needed it."

"Why?"

"I thought..."

Virginia started to step forward, but Richard's hand was quicker. "Not yet," he whispered.

"Why did you need it? Are you drinking again?"

The man stumbled forward, reaching for Joy, but she'd already backed away from him. "I've read these tombstones over and over again," he said, stopping again in front of her, "and prayed over them, hoping something would come to me about the jewelry box; anything. And then one day I thought to check the old neighborhood. I went inside that house and he had it. It didn't belong to him but he had it. Didn't have the key."

"And so you broke it open."

Once again, the flashlight traveled up and down the girl's form. "Yes."

"You destroyed it!"

"Destroyed what? Just some old..."

"Whatever you found in there was my mother's heart, and grandmother's heart, and I can't believe it! I hate you! I hate you!"

The girl reached for her father's coat and Virginia and Richard moved forward. Virginia could feel the wetness of the snow. She'd worn her tennis shoes and the water had finally traveled beyond the fabric and past her socks. She could feel Richard's breath behind her.

Suddenly, a blast of light hit her eyes. She covered them quickly but the beam remained.

"What are you doing here? Who are you?" Tom demanded.

"Friends, friends of Joy!"

Joy still held her father's coat sleeve. He wrenched it away. "I knew she couldn't be alone!" he hollered, stumbling away from her. "Leave me alone! It was just a book, an old book your mother kept when she was young, a journal she kept when she was dating me. And another, one of your grandmother's. I read them both. I didn't find the money."

"What money?" Joy asked.

"The money I thought your mother had kept from me," he mumbled. "All those years...And when I needed it she wouldn't give it to me, and so I finally left her. 'Deal with life on your own,' I said to her. I chucked the jewelry box hoping the spring would loosen the lid, but it didn't. It hit the floor and flew under the couch. I looked at your mother. She was in pain but I didn't care. I needed that money."

Virginia could smell the alcohol on his breath. The man's coat was worn and his clothes torn, showing exposed flesh on his knees. He was unshaven, his dark beard with a hint of gray covering most of his face. She clicked off her flashlight. "Where are you staying?" Virginia asked.

"None of your concern," Tom replied, kneeling at the graves.

"Where are MY journals?" Joy asked hotly.

"In my car, over there." He pointed a dirty coat sleeve.

"Your car..."

"Since I don't have a home to speak of, or a place to sleep..." He buried his head nearer the tombstones and allowed the tears to flow. "All this time..."

"I can't believe you, Father. I can't believe that you'd do this to Mother." Joy was like a scared deer, her eyes large, her voice suddenly small. It was if she was waiting...for something.

The man stood. "I did nothing to your mother. And it's just too bad you can't ask her to tell you what she did to me. You were just a child, believed everything she said."

"You...left us," the girl squeaked. "Just left us at the house. Mom went crazy for days, drinking, passing out on the couch. I was all alone."

"Serves you right," Tom muttered as he stood to look at her. Virginia held the girl close, and Richard was suddenly standing next to Joy on the other side; or had he been there all along?

"That's no way to speak to your daughter," he said.

"Perhaps not." The man swallowed. "Let me get the diaries." He hobbled from them and as Virginia watched she felt the girl relax. The tension increased as he returned.

"So where is your mother buried?" he asked, handing the girl two worn books. One had a blue cover, the other a silver-white.

"Thank you," Joy muttered, holding the books close to her heart. "Mother is at another cemetery."

"I figured that part out, but could never understand it."

117

"Why?" The girl was visibly shaking now but she stood her ground. Virginia's heart pounded.

"Why wasn't she buried by her parents? I looked everywhere for her, in every cemetery. Nothing."

"*Safe Haven* was our home, Father. We had no other relatives. We didn't even have *you*! Mother...she died alone because of you. She was all alone, and they couldn't find me, and they put her in a grave with only a number on it, and it's all your fault, your fault!"

The man blinked. "All alone? Where?"

"By the freeway near the park."

"Away from you?"

"She...she wanted a better life for me."

"And so she left you?"

It was all Virginia could do to remain silent, but the words had to be worked through, all of them, including the words burning in her own heart.

"She was sick."

"You mean she was a drunk."

A shudder crept down Virginia's arms and moved through the fabric of her coat.

"She tried to take care of me, really," Joy began, "but without money, and being sick she..."

"She was *no good*, you need to know that."

"She was my mother."

"And I am your father."

The girl began to sob. She held Virginia's arm even more tightly.

The man walked closer. Virginia was cold and her feet burned. Richard finally spoke and it was just like him. He always waited to say just the right words at just the right time; and the time, evidently, had come.

"We plan on adopting Joy," he said. "Now that we know you're alive..."

The man coughed. "So that's it," he said. "You came all this way just to see me so that I could sign the papers. Well, I've been to *Safe Haven* and I've met the woman Jean." He smiled a sickly smile that made Virginia wince. "Of course, she didn't know it was me..." He looked down at Joy. "So, daughter, how about walking your good old dad to the car?"

"Where's the jewelry box?" Joy asked. Virginia hadn't looked at her cell phone in some time. What was it, 2 a.m.?

"You don't want that old thing."

"Give it to me and I'll go with you," she said.

"What? And leave these...fine people?"

"I need that box. Take me with you. Now."

"You sound just like your mother," he drawled. "Come, this way," he motioned, but Virginia's arm remained taut. "You are not going," she said.

"We will not let you go with that man," echoed Richard, taking her other arm. "You've got the diaries, what could you possibly want with a broken down jewelry box?"

"My mother's heart."

"Come on." Tom reached for her, and this time his fingertips brushed her coat.

Virginia drew the girl close. "You can't – go. We need you."

"Not as much as my father does. Look at him. I can take care of him and once he's sober he'll want to give me the box, and then everything will be okay. You'll see."

Richard turned the girl's chin upward. Even in the surrounding darkness, Virginia could see her small mouth trembling. "When will you come home?" he asked.

"I don't know," she replied, her breath stinging the air. "But...oh, I love you both!" Thin arms wrapped around them and then she was gone.

***

Days later the thought occurred to Virginia that the girl, Joy, now so very close to being a woman, might never return to them. She would get the box, Virginia was sure of that, but would she be able to leave her father?

She'd heard countless stories about children wanting to return to neglectful or abusive parents only to be neglected or abused again. It seemed a natural thing for children to be with a parent no matter how terrible the natural parent was. And so was the case with Joy.

The yellow journal, that's all she and Richard had.

It appeared to Virginia that life was never what she planned and no matter how she worked at it, the struggle was still the same. The stones - Listening, Trust, Optimism, Tenacity and Constancy - still sat as before on her mantel; and she looked at them every day. The stone of trust would occasionally turn black, just opposite of the stone of constancy which was as clear as a spring morning that was quickly turning into summer. Not surprisingly, she was constantly finding the black stone digging holes where holes shouldn't be, and the clear stone reminding her of her constancy with God.

And then she'd think of Joy.

Jean Rasmussen had been angry at the news. And she'd been angry at them. But the law was the law. If Joy was really with her father, there was nothing the shelter could do unless the father gave them just cause. The man named Tom Sorensen had never been seen after leaving his wife and child, but he had every right to her - at least until she turned eighteen. There was nothing any one of them could do.

The Gift

It was nearing September. Almost a year had passed since the death of their little one. Beatrice was always on her mind, though most of her thoughts during the year had been about Joy. Oh, Joy, another girl lost, then found, then lost again.

The small lavender room was still empty, and maybe the space was as it should be. She was happy with Richard; happy with him and their small lives together. Perhaps they would never have children. Perhaps not having them was the way God wanted it.

She'd not quite resigned herself to the empty space; she wasn't angry anymore about what she didn't have. Rather, she was grateful for what she had. Richard. He was a blessing to her life. He loved her. And she loved him.

The leaves were just beginning to turn.

"Can you take me to Beatrice's grave?" she asked one Sunday after church, and Richard reached his warm arm around her.

It's about time, he could have said, but didn't. Instead, he walked her to the car and they drove to the same cemetery that Joy's mother had been buried in. Funny, she hadn't even thought of the connection between the two, she hadn't seen the spot where the precious babe had been laid to rest, so it was no wonder.

Or was it a wonder? How could she have gone all of this time and not asked Richard the question? "So where is she?" she asked now, her heart beating quickly, her hands wetting, her mouth going dry. She couldn't do this.

"Funny you should ask, but I think I'll keep you guessing until we get there," he answered, turning on the ignition. And so they drove. At the cemetery entrance, Richard stopped the car. "Are you sure you're ready?" he asked.

"It's been a year," she answered quietly. "Don't you think it's time?"

He nodded, and as the car wove through the rows of orange and yellow trees along the cemetery path, Richard stopped. The car rested some ten feet from where Grace was buried!

"She's behind that tree," Richard said, pointing to a place just north of them. She looked and the view was breathtaking. Blue skies, little pinwheels perched on white sticks, flags blowing, tombstones standing as if at attention.

He took her hand. She wondered if he'd noticed the dampness that had accumulated there as well as on her face, but he said nothing. They walked through the crisp grass. As the sunlight streamed against her cheeks she thought she felt Beatrice near her. Such a little girl with such a big smile.

A small tear escaped her eye. She brushed it with her left hand and continued with Richard. A few yards later they had reached the tombstone. She looked down.

Beatrice Stone: Our Little Angel
Born: December 4.
Died: September 25.
She will always be in our hearts.

The little white headstone glittered in the sunlight. "It's beautiful," she said, placing the small daisies she'd found on the roadside near her daughter's name. The tears came freely now. "She was our beautiful little daughter."

"Still is and always will be," said Richard, squeezing her hand.

"I know. But it's not the same without her."

They stood for a long time after that, listening to the birds that had somehow found their way to the shade of the trees. The cars rushed by on the busy street to the east, and the other well-wishers, just a few, continued to journey to the cemetery on this already warming day.

Virginia adjusted her sweater, then decided at the last minute to tie it around her waist before asking her husband the question that hovered in her mind. "So," she said at last, "our little girl and Joy's neglectful mother are buried near each other."

"Don't call her that."

"What?"

"Neglectful. Grace Sorenson had...problems because she was sick."

Virginia shrugged. "I can't believe we allowed Joy to leave with her father."

"What else were we supposed to do? I didn't see you trying to stop her."

"I know." She shrugged again. "I wish we'd dragged her back to the shelter. Now we'll never see her again."

"We can't be sure of that. She came back once before."

Virginia thought about the moment and it was like yesterday. The way Joy looked - dirty and unkept. A small lump entered her throat and tears welled in her eyes. "This stinks," she said. "Where is God now, now that we truly need him?"

Richard turned to her. "Do you really think God has abandoned us?"

She nodded, but in the nod she knew she was lying. God would never abandon her.

"God is here, can't you feel him? Close your eyes. Can't you feel him?"

"Church is getting to you," she said, but she closed her eyes anyway and felt the warm breeze caress her face and cheeks. "It's just the sun," she said.

"Yes, it's the Son," he answered, still taking in the newness of the sky.

***

A week later the package arrived. A small box sat on the doorstep, just as she and Richard were leaving to go to church. She picked it up and looked down at the lid. Tears sprang to her eyes but she didn't open it. Not yet.

"Richard, come quick!" she yelled as she peered down at it. Oh, how the thing gave her hope!

"What is it?" Richard asked, peering over her shoulder. "Oh."

Inside was a key, Joy's key, and with it a little note. Virginia picked up the note written on the corner of something, it looked like an old envelope.

"This is just to help you to remember who you are. I think of you every day. Joy."

Virginia removed the key from the box. She held it up against the light. It was the first time she'd seen the key close up, and it appeared to be made of iron, plated with nickel; sections of the key had worn off so she could see the layers. The bow, or place of holding, was a sort of shamrock shape, and the barrel was short, the tooth at the end, small and simple.

Although the key was old the chain was quite new and was of basic design.

"Why don't you wear it?" Richard offered, taking it from her fingers and placing it around her neck. Virginia could feel the warmth of it almost instantly as it fell against her skin.

She looked out. It was cold, especially in the mornings, but Joy had been here regardless and she'd left this small gift. "How do you think she's doing with her father?" she hesitantly asked.

Her husband looked out and followed her eyes where they searched; there was only one faraway cloud clinging to the already blue sky. "I worry about her, but I try not to," he said, reaching an arm around her shoulders.

"Me, too. Are you ready?" she asked.

He turned, locked up the house, and together they walked to the car.

***

Near the end of October, the leaves gracing the roads and lawns had been covered by snow. And a month later, Virginia was dreading another Christmas without her little girl; without Joy. *Joy to the World.* It seemed a funny song, now that time was passing by without a child, without a teen to fill her heart.

But she had Richard, and with all of her heart she loved him. What wasn't there to love? He wasn't perfect by any means, but he was good to her - so good to her. The business was growing as well, and Virginia had begun her classes again. Most days, the lavender room was empty, but occasionally, like today, she'd find the cozy chair, a good book - sometimes even The *Good Book* - and read. Time would pass and Virginia would recall for a time the painful moments and what they had taught her: About life, about death, about continuing forward.

Listening to God was better than living life without him, she knew that now, although it wasn't often easy to take his advice. How well she remembered the last time. He'd stood in this very room and peered down at her as she'd read. She didn't see him, but she knew he was there, watching and helping her as he had always done.

And then Richard had entered. "Good book?" he'd asked. He was still wearing the apron that he'd purchased for her and was holding a silver bowl.

127

"What have you got in there?" she asked.

"Chocolate. God told me it was time to give you some chocolate."

She laughed.

"I'm serious. I almost heard him, too. 'Virginia is feeling sad,' he said. 'Make her something sweet.' And so, wa-la! Here I am."

"Here you are," said Virginia. "The book is good," she added, realizing she hadn't answered his question.

"What is it?"

"Raising a Teenager." She held up the book.

Now it was his turn to laugh. And then he grew solemn. "So, you expect her back soon?"

"Oh, I don't know about soon," said Virginia, waving him over so that she could lick the bowl. There was a wooden spoon in it, which Virginia pulled out. "But I think..." She took another taste, "I think it will be soon. And if not..."

"If not?"

She peered up into Richard's eyes. A fine line of chocolate was just under his chin. So, he'd snuck a bit before coming into the room. She smiled, tears forming in her blue eyes. "I have been filled with such a deep peace these last few days," she said.

Richard squatted next to the chair, the same chair that had rocked the new little one that had left them like a breeze. He placed the bowl on the carpet next to him. "I have been feeling pretty good, myself," he said, "but I figured it had to do with us going to church together."

"And reading the Bible," said Virginia. "And praying."

The Gift – A Parable of the Key

"It isn't as if we have just been sitting around waiting for God to answer us," said Richard, touching her lightly on the arm.

"We've been busy," added Virginia. "And besides..." She took her husband's arm and pulled him closer to her. "...Joy is a strong girl. She will take care of her father, and one day she will return home to us."

"Are you really that sure?"

"If not..." Virginia smiled again and Richard leaned in. The smell of his aftershave wafted to her nostrils and reminded her once again of the mountains where they'd been married, and where, on another early spring day he'd proposed to her once again.

***

The announcement arrived that morning, almost two weeks before Christmas. John was dead.

She and Richard had visited him only occasionally since Joy's departure from their lives, but even in those times John would blink and then he'd remember who they both were, though sometimes it took some doing to get him to that point.

How well she remembered their last visit.

"So you've come to sell me pots and pans," he'd muttered under his breath. "I don't need none." They stood on the porch, she, her husband, and the man who was always forgetting things. Once he remembered, he would ask them about Joy and about her mother; where was she anyway?

They would tell him she was dead and he would remember. A small tear would crease his left eye, or his right, and his hands would fumble for something to wipe his eyes.

It was always and forever the same.

Except for today. The funeral was Saturday, their busiest day at *Just Desserts*, but they had to go; both of them. At the back of her mind Virginia wondered if Joy would somehow make it, and if so, if they'd have a moment or two to visit. She didn't say anything to Richard.

But by the time Saturday had come and gone, including the funeral, with a *no appearance* by Joy or her father, Virginia knew the truth, or at least, she thought she knew it. Joy was merely wrapped up in caring for her father.

Whenever she was around the park, the freeway or *Safe Haven*, she would take a second or a third look, just to be sure. She'd talked to Jean only twice since Joy had gone back to live with her father, and Jean hadn't seen the girl, which, she said *made her sad to even think about.*

As for Virginia, she tried not to dwell on the sadness, but what God had given them both. She was deep in thought about this very thing when she heard a knock at the door. It was just two days before Christmas.

Virginia blinked. "So, you've come to the door this time," she said.

"I have a message."

Virginia ushered God in. Richard peered from the couch, stood, and met them at the front door.

"So how are you doing today?" God asked, extending his hand.

"Fine, fine."

"And you, Virginia? How are you doing?"

"Good. And you, God?"

God smiled, and the brightness of his smile filled the room and added to the glow of the Christmas tree. "Well, I'll be. What a beautiful tree." He left them and walked closer to it.

Virginia and Richard had decorated the tree extra special this year. The homemade ornaments had been saved from their childhoods, and now graced the green tree along with glittering white lights. An uneven star topped the tree - a star Richard had made when he was only six. It was made of cardboard and glitter, most of which had already rubbed itself off.

"I remember the year you made that," said God. "You had just lost your mother."

Richard blinked.

"How...I mean, yes, that was a hard year."

God turned and all Virginia could think about was the little Richard had spoken about his mother. She didn't know much - only that his mother had gotten sick, after which his father had followed close behind. Within weeks he was buried alongside her. It was sometimes like that when the grief was too great.

Like herself, Richard had spent much time with his grandmother; in fact, she had raised him after that. What she knew of the star wasn't much, only that he'd made it that year; and his grandmother had made such a fuss over it that she'd put the new star she'd recently purchased back in its box, and it had remained there until she died.

"And you, Virginia..." God looked to the center of the tree where she had hung the Santa Claus ornament made of clay that she had also painted in school. Most, but not all of the paint had worn off.

"I can't believe it," God said, reaching for the memory and holding it up in his palm. "The day you painted this, do you remember what happened?"

Virginia shrugged. "I was in school."

"Yes, and the teacher, a Ms. Graham, as I remember, complimented you on such fine craftsmanship."

Virginia might have blushed, but her heart had quickened. Why would such a simple, long ago memory make her heart race?

Still holding the ornament, God caressed it lightly. "The colors have faded, but I can still see the beauty."

Virginia reached for it. "It's pretty ugly now," she said, taking the gem in her hand. Tears filled her eyes though she did not know why.

"Not ugly, just growing to perfection," God said. "Like the stones, this symbol of life can teach you many things. I've been to see Joy," he said.

Virginia was still holding the Santa Claus ornament. She released it now and watched the little man swing back and forth, back and forth, on the extended branch. When the ornament had stopped swaying, she finally had the courage to look up at God.

She wasn't sure why she suddenly felt like she'd need courage to look up just then, but as their eyes met she somehow knew that the news God had for her was not good.

"Joy. She's dead," Virginia said.

The Gift – A Parable of the Key

God reached for her. Holding her within his arms he began to whisper. His voice was like the stillness of a lake in spring. "She is alive," he said. "But she has been hurt." Still in God's arms she felt his hands caress her hair. "She was in a fire."

"What?" Richard's voice was a flame as it passed by her ears. "A fire? When?"

"Just yesterday."

Virginia looked up at God. Tears streamed down his own cheeks. "She needs you," he said.

***

Virginia tried not to think about the last time she'd been in this hospital with her friend, Paul, but the memories of that time in her life came flooding back the moment she stepped through the door. She remembered another time, when, anxious to get the new babe that had just been born, she'd raced up the hallway only to find that the little one had already left this earth.

Nurses surrounded them, and the smell of antiseptic filled her nostrils as she thought about Joy and all that God had told them. It was unbelievable really. Why would a man start an old abandoned house on fire with his daughter inside?

But he was drunk, and *people do things they might not usually do, when they have been drinking,* God had told them; Virginia and Richard raced through their house for coats and shoes and the keys to the car. Only when the front door had been safely locked behind them had Virginia noticed the tree in the window.

It was still lit.

Richard held her hand. They did not speak, they ran, and once the room was found they didn't knock, they went inside. Joy's father was by the bed. They couldn't see his face, only his greasy hair, his clothing hanging limp and dirty around his arms. They did not speak to him.

Joy's face was covered in white bandages, as also, sections of her arms. Her legs, probably covered with the same white material lay hidden underneath the blanket. Only her eyes showed. She appeared to be asleep.

The man was sobbing.

Virginia's heart pounded. She was angry, but she could not speak. *Joy!*

Walking to the other side of the bed she peered at her daughter, for surely, this was the daughter that had always been meant for them. This...this...man didn't deserve her!

Virginia almost spoke then, as the stillness filled her mind and heart; it was almost like death had surrounded her, taken in her very soul and had come back for more.

She remembered God's words. "She needs you," he had said. And she had felt those words even as they had pierced her soul. She'd known then what she must do.

"How long?" she asked the man on the other side of the bed.

"Since she arrived. I'm sorry," he added, pressing his face against the sheets.

"How much of her body?"

134

The man didn't look at her. "They say almost half."

"Will she see?"

The man looked up from his weeping. "Who are you?" he asked. His face was streaked with dirty tears, the same sort of tears Virginia had seen only months ago when Joy had returned to them only to be taken away again.

"We're her parents," she answered, and the man blinked, once, and then buried his head again in the sheets. "I'm sorry," he said again.

Richard reached for her hand. She held it tightly, even as she wept.

A day later, even before Joy awoke from the deep sleep the fire had brought upon her, Richard had discovered the jewelry box. It sat, mended somehow, on the silver tray that served as Joy's end table. For the first time Virginia was able to trace the engravings on the box.

On the front she could see small houses, a couple of engraved trees and swans in the forefront, taking a leisurely swim on the lake. Turning the box in her hands, Virginia could see that on the right side of the box, it appeared the same swan was standing as if waiting for a swim. At the back of the box a couple held each other in a loving embrace, their home and trees in the distance; the left side showed the same swan, now swimming next to the reeds within the lake called home.

The hole where the key entered was cracked, though some gluing had again put the box in order. She didn't look inside.

They'd spent hours in the hospital before Joy finally regained consciousness and during that time Virginia and Richard had learned some frightening things. Though Joy's heart had been monitored as well as her breathing, and even though she'd been hooked up to an IV and her pain had been treated with morphine, the biggest shock came in the form of what had become of her belt and her shoes. Not only had the fire melted them off of her, she'd had to have dead skin washed from her wounds so that the extent of her injuries could be determined. Joy's face had received superficial burns, but those on her arms and legs had been third degree.

Virginia hadn't spoken with Joy's father. As she watched him, still in his pitiful state, she decided that, at least for the time being, she would remain silent. As Richard sat next to her, his arm around her shoulders, waist, and taking her hand upon occasion, Virginia couldn't help but be grateful.

How could she do any of this without Him? Without God?

Even now, as she continued to watch her daughter in the bed (she'd gone to sleep again) she couldn't help but remember her beautiful green eyes upon awakening.

"Mom, is that you?"

The girl's eyes blinked open, a tiny mouth revealed through the white cloth. The doctor had told them that because she was young and hadn't inhaled too much smoke, which might have damaged her airways, she could speak.

Virginia blinked back the tears, but that did not stop them from falling down her cheeks. Joy had never called her Mom before. She reached for a bandaged hand, and then thought better of it. Instead, she peered closer at the green eyes that lay blinking before her.

"What happened?" Joy asked. "I feel so strange."

"You're in the hospital. A fire began in the house; you were asleep..."

Joy's eyes tightened shut. A small tear was released. "My father, is he here?" she asked, her eyes still closed, the small tear wetting the white fabric.

"Yes."

"I want him out...out..."she said, not turning.

"Joy..." The man's voice was like a hollow tube. "You can't mean that. I..."

"I can. Out," she said again.

***

"He's gone."

Virginia looked down the hall as if Joy's father might still turn the corner at any minute. She didn't know if she could hold her anger in any longer. She didn't know how much longer she could hold the pain that was filling her soul for Joy.

What would Joy's life be like, now that she'd experienced the mental and physical pain of fire searing through her body? How could she live, knowing her father had caused her pain?

She swallowed. "Where is he?" she asked.

Richard took her hand. They were in the hospital waiting room. It was late. Other than a few couples at the other end of the room, they were alone.

"He has gone to a hotel. I gave him some money."

"You what?"

"He had nowhere to go!"

"After what he did to Joy?"

"He's a human being who has made a terrible mistake. He needed a place to sleep."

"So he was drunk," she said, not daring to look into his eyes for fear of what she might find there - sympathy, some sort of love for a man who had scarred their daughter for life.

"He was cooking in the abandoned house. A grease fire. He says he must have passed out. When he woke up Joy was screaming in the room just off the kitchen. He went to her and somehow managed to douse the fire. She'd been sleeping on the couch."

"He should be in jail."

"Probably. But right now we need to think of Joy."

The lump rose in Virginia's throat. "I'm sorry," she said, "I'm just so angry...at him. I'm just so worried about Joy."

"I know."

***

Weeks later, Joy's wounds were healing and closing. She'd also been through some rehabilitation. Reconstructive surgery would come next, followed by counseling, and integrating Joy into her new life.

Joy's father was in jail. It happened within the week as more was learned about the fire that had completely gutted the old shack. His drinking was completely out of hand; an understatement according to Virginia, and much therapy was needed before he would be able to step back into civilized society.

Joy was constantly in pain; she writhed at times on the hospital bed, even though she had been given drugs to keep the pain at bay. More medication was given before a dressing change or when she went in for physical therapy, but the pain was still there. Virginia could see it in the girl's eyes, even when she wasn't moaning or crying out because of it.

The tub room was the worst, and the tweezers used to pull off dead skin ran a close second.

Virginia, when she was not in the room with Joy, sat alone or with Richard in the hospital chapel. It was quiet there, and much too neglected in her opinion. She prayed there and thought about God and all he'd done for her. How would he help Joy now?

She could feel him, although his presence since leaving their home, had escaped her. But she knew that he was there, watching over her as well as Joy. She didn't have to see God to know that.

Just five days after the accident, doctors took care of the burns on Joy's left arm and began grafting the skin from her thighs. More grafts continued, and for Virginia, more visits to the chapel were necessary. She'd never felt as close to God as she did in those long weeks following the accident.

Bible reading had become a necessity along with prayer and speaking to Joy whenever she could, encouraging her to keep moving forward with hope and faith. Three weeks later, it was time for Joy to take her first short walk in the hospital hallway.

But Joy was afraid.

She sat on the edge of her bed, her legs draped over the side like limp towels. "Blood is coming out through my skin, blood is coming out!" she screamed. "What if I can't stand? What if my legs break?"

"Just hold onto the walker," the nurse counseled her, "and push up. Your arms will support you when you begin to push forward. I will be here if you need me."

Richard placed a firm hand against Virginia's back. She tried to breathe.

"You can do it, Joy," she echoed.

Richard smiled at her. "You're tough," he said, and Virginia wondered, in that moment, if Richard was speaking of her or of their daughter, but it didn't matter. All of them would have to be tough the next few months to get through this.

Joy looked at him and Virginia thought she smiled. "Okay, but you'll be here to catch me if I fall?"

When the nurse nodded, Joy gripped the walker and slowly, as if her legs were truly made of Jell-O, stood. For a few moments she wobbled, but still held tight to the walker.

"Now, take your first step," said the nurse.

A short step followed, and then another. When Joy had managed five, she began to cry.

"I can't believe it. I did it!"

"And you'll do many more things," said the nurse, as they returned her to her bed.

***

The Gift – A Parable of the Key

The day Joy asked for a mirror, Virginia wondered what she should say to her. She'd already brought over the old jewelry box which the girl had promptly opened using the key Virginia still wore around her neck.

Inside were the two diaries - one was Joy's mother's, the other, her grandmother's, and something else. She reached in to retrieve it.

Joy held up a framed picture. She turned it. It was a picture of her mother and someone else, older surely, but still beautiful.

Joy caressed the picture's face. "Grandmother was just as beautiful as mother was," she began. "Will I be beautiful, too?"

A large lump grew in Virginia's throat. Her eyes filled with tears. "You will always be beautiful," she said.

"The doctors, they said the fire got to my legs and arms pretty good, but my face was looking better. I don't see what they mean," she added, tears forming in her eyes. "What's all this red stuff? Will it go away? Will I have...scars?"

Virginia blinked. Though some redness and scabs remained, Joy's face was healing nicely. They had been in the hospital all of three weeks, and the doctors were already talking about a release.

Joy placed the mirror on the bed. "I think I'm ready to go," she said. "Can you feel it? It's almost like my mother and grandmother are here, you know? It's almost as if they're saying, 'You can do it. Just remember who you are.' You know what that means, don't you?"

"That you should always think highly of yourself," said Virginia.

"That you shouldn't give up," added Richard.

"Yeah, sure. But that's not the most important part." Taking the jewelry box again into her hands and stroking the sides just like the old man had done, she looked inside. "I am God's child. That's who I am."

Afterword

The tree was still lit, although Christmas had ended almost four weeks prior. The gifts were still gathered around the tree and the spirit within the room was as real as if it was still Christmas day.

And perhaps it was, at least for Virginia, Richard, and Joy.

One gift in particular sat near the back of the tree until the very end. It was dressed in white with a red bow. The key hung where the tag might have been.

"This is for you," Virginia said.

The girl's face glowed. She was healing well and the short few days the family had spent at home would be remembered. Her face, though a splotchy red, was looking better. It would be some time before she healed completely, both emotionally and physically, but she was making good progress. Virginia, looking at their daughter now, knew she could do it. Richard was smiling, eager for the red bow to be removed along with the white paper. Virginia was just as eager.

What would Joy think?

"You guys, you've bought me too much already," she said, taking the ribbon in her delicate hands and pulling at the strands. "I love this paper," she said suddenly. "It's white, like God's flowing robe."

Virginia touched her lips and tried to hold in the tears, a lump forming in her throat.

"Tear the paper," Richard coaxed, but the girl placed her delicate forefinger under every piece of tape and lifted each flap with her charred hands. She had regained much movement in her fingers as well as her legs; but there was a long way to go. There were still dressing changes, rehabilitation and a topographical suit she'd need to wear day and night to flatten out the scars on various places on her chest, arms, and legs. She couldn't use the stairs, either, but was walking more every day. The coming year still held many challenges.

The paper removed, she sat it beside her. "I have no idea what this is," she said, smiling at them both. "But whatever it is, I will love it," she said, "just as I love you."

Virginia begin to sob then, and Richard, for the first time since she'd first met him, had fresh tears rolling down his own cheeks.

Joy opened the lid. Inside was a piece of paper. She lifted it out and began to read:

Certificate of Adoption
This is to certify that
Joy Sorenson
Has been formally adopted
into the *Stone* family

signed by *Jean Rasmussen*
On this 24th Day of
December 2015

Safe Haven Community

Kathryn Elizabeth Jones

Dear Reader,

Thank you so much for purchasing *The Gift: A Parable of the Key*. In case you're unaware, this is the final book in the Parable series, and the last book I will be writing about Virginia Bean.

This saddens me. As an author, you want your characters to live on, but the time comes when new projects are in the making in which you're drawn to. And there is one drawing my attention now. The good news is that you can begin the series again with *Conquering Your Goliaths: A Parable of the Five Stones*, and then travel to *The Feast: A Parable of the Ring* without even leaving your home.

I hope you do.

When I wrote *Conquering Your Goliaths*, I had no idea that the book would turn into a series. But when you have a husband like I do, who gently nudges you on to the next book, it's all you can do but move forward to the next.

Virginia is a lot like me, and an awful lot unlike me. I appreciate what she's taught me about God and about not only conquering my own goliaths, but reaching for that joy that only comes through service to others.

I appreciate all of the reviews I've received on my books thus far. As many of you know, I also write mystery and Christian nonfiction. Every review is priceless to me, even if it isn't as positive as I would like. As an author, I am also on a journey; a journey of self-discovery and creativity. I learn as I write and I get better as I write.

Will you review *The Gift*? And if you haven't done so already, will you review *Conquering Your Goliaths* and *The Feast*?

Thank you so much.

I am always open to emails from readers, so feel free to write and share your thoughts about God, about my books, or anything else the books have brought to your mind and heart.

With Love,

Kathryn

kathy@ariverofstones.com

Amazon Page:
http://www.amazon.com/author/joneskathryn

Twitter handle: @kakido

Facebook page:
http://www.facebook.com/kathrynelizabethjones.author

Blog:
http://www.ariverofstones.com